"R.J. Patterson does a fantastic job at keeping you engaged and interested. I look forward to more from this talented author."

- Aaron Patterson
bestselling author of SWEET DREAMS

DEAD SHOT

"Small town life in southern Idaho might seem quaint and idyllic to some. But when local newspaper reporter Cal Murphy begins to un-cover a series of strange deaths that are linked to a sticky spider web of deception, the lid on the peaceful town is blown wide open. Told with all the energy and bravado of an old pro, first-timer R.J. Patterson hits one out of the park his first time at bat with *Dead Shot*. It's that good."

- Vincent Zandri
bestselling author of THE REMAINS

"You can tell R.J. knows what it's like to live in the newspaper world, but with *Dead Shot*, he's proven that he also can write one heck of a murder mystery."

- Josh Katzowitz
NFL writer for CBSSports.com
& author of Sid Gillman: Father of the Passing Game

"Patterson has a mean streak about a mile wide and puts his two main characters through quite a horrible ride, which makes for good reading."

- Richard D., reader

DEAD LINE

"This book kept me on the edge of my seat the whole time. I didn't really want to put it down. R.J. Patterson has hooked me. I'll be back for more."

- Bob Behler
3-time Idaho broadcaster of the year
and play-by-play voice for Boise State football

"Like a John Grisham novel, from the very start I was pulled right into the story and couldn't put the book down. It was as if I personally knew and cared about what happened to each of the main characters. Every chapter ended with so much excitement and suspense I had to continue to read until I learned how it ended, even though it kept me up until 3:00 A.M.

*- **Ray F.**, reader*

DEAD IN THE WATER

"In Dead in the Water, R.J. Patterson accurately captures the action-packed saga of a what could be a real-life college football scandal. The sordid details will leave readers flipping through the pages as fast as a hurry-up offense."

- Mark Schlabach,
ESPN college sports columnist and
co-author of *Called to Coach*
and *Heisman: The Man Behind the Trophy*

THE WARREN OMISSIONS

"What can be more fascinating than a super high concept novel that reopens the conspiracy behind the JFK assassination while the threat of a global world war rests in the balance? With his new novel, *The Warren Omissions*, former journalist turned bestselling author R.J. Patterson proves he just might be the next worthy successor to Vince Flynn."

*- **Vincent Zandri***
bestselling author of THE REMAINS

NO WAY

OUT

A Brady Hawk novel

R.J.
PATTERSON

For John Moore, a great friend and
an even better man

CHAPTER 1

Cuevita, Colombia

BRADY HAWK PULLED UP on a low-hanging branch and ascended the acacia tree with relative ease. Locating a sturdy limb three-fourths of the way up the trunk, he set up his perch. He pulled out his binoculars to make sure he had a clear line of sight on where the alleged deal was supposed to occur. Once he confirmed his position was optimum, all he could do was wait for darkness to settle over the jungle and Al Hasib agents to engage with the arms dealer pedaling an intercontinental ballistic missile.

Hawk glanced at his right hand steadying him on the branch and watched as an ant crawled nearby. The insect almost seemed disinterested in the presence of a human as it meandered across Hawk's hand—right up until he felt the searing pain of a bite. Hawk flicked the ant away and turned his attention back toward the meeting place. The area remained devoid of people and any activity.

"Are you sure the intel is good on this one?" Hawk asked over his communication device.

"Getting bored out there?" Alex Duncan asked. "You're only in one of the most beautiful jungles in the world."

"Tell that to my itching hand."

"Mosquitoes?"

"Ants. They look like little ninjas, and their bites pack quite a punch."

"If only there was something I could do," Alex said, sarcasm dripping in her voice.

Hawk grunted. "Just trying to make small talk and stay focused. Staring at a clearing in the jungle for several hours isn't all it's cracked up to be."

"I'm not sure anyone ever said—"

"Wait," Hawk said. "I think I see some movement."

He peered through his binoculars and saw a large transport truck rumbling across the forest floor.

"Is that it?" Alex asked.

"I've got eyes on the target."

"Well, get ready because they're going to want to point that thing at somebody after they figure out what we did. If you're the closest target . . ."

Hawk didn't need Alex to explain the situation any further. He knew just how dangerous his mission was, which ranged anywhere from captured by extremist Muslim terrorists to annihilated by a missile. No outcome seemed satisfactory to Hawk, except for the one he went to Colombia to achieve: Stop the sale of an Intercontinental Ballistic Missile (ICBM) to Al Hasib and return to the U.S. with one of the men associated with German arms dealer Dietrich Oberfelk.

The thrum of insects and sounds of other nocturnal animals filling up the night air paused briefly due to the grumbling diesel engine that invaded the territory. The brakes squeaked as the monstrous vehicle slowed to a stop. After a few seconds, the doors to the truck's cabin swung open and a half dozen armed men spilled out. Moving with precision, they circled the truck and inspected the weapon.

Hawk shook his head in disbelief that a weapon that size had found its way into the jungle without a pursuing entourage.

"How did they get that thing in here?" Hawk asked aloud.

"You're in Colombia," Alex answered. "Grease a few palms, customs agents look the other way."

"But they had to drive this thing on the road. If a missile this size was just cruising down the road in the U.S.—"

"It'd be all over social media, right?" Alex interrupted. "That's why we don't transport weapons that way."

"I know, but it's just—it's just astounding."

"Don't get too caught up in your fan boy moment. You still have a mission to accomplish."

"Roger that," Hawk said.

The infrared function on his binoculars had been rendered ineffective due to the headlights from the truck and the bulbs ringing the flatbed. No one could sneak up on the arms deal without getting caught in the beams of what Hawk figured was enough wattage to illuminate a soccer field.

He trained his glasses on the sole entrance into the clearing. When the Firestorm team learned about the proposed arms deal from U.S. Army intelligence, the exchange was schedule to occur at 23:00.

Two more minutes.

General Van Fortner had notified Firestorm head J.D. Blunt about the deal almost immediately after receiving the intel. While U.S. troops held a constant presence in the Colombian jungles aiding the South American nation in ferreting out drug lords, Fortner wanted to more than eliminate the threat of Al Hasib volleying a missile at an east coast metropolis. Fortner wanted a prisoner. And prisoners complicated matters when official military action was undertaken. But Firestorm? There was nothing official about them, still identified as Project X on the Department of Defense's line item budget.

Hawk understood how critical—and danger-ous—his mission was to the overall success of putting an end to Oberfelk's activities on the illegal weapons market. Without an arms seller, many of the terrorist cells would resort to more desperate measures to seize weapons, forcing the usually hidden enemy into the open for easier removal.

"How do things look on your end?" Alex asked.

"Still waiting for Al Hasib."

"You won't have to wait long. I'm watching them on satellite now. They're about thirty seconds away, so get ready."

"Roger that."

Hawk pulled out his rifle and peered through the scope. Swinging from left to right, he put in his sights Oberfelk's half dozen guards and refrained from pulling the trigger. To do so might have made sense under normal operational procedures, but this mission was anything but normal. Hawk caught the glint of headlights through the trees just ahead of an en-tourage of trucks lumbering up to the semi holding the ICBM.

Hawk watched as representatives from the two groups approached one another and shook hands. They exchanged some papers before walking over to one of the Al Hasib trucks and opening up their lap-tops. They set their computers on the hood, and Hawk watched one of the men hammer away on the keyboard. Seconds later, he was hammering away on the fender with his fists.

"Something's wrong," Hawk said with a hint of satisfaction. "Did you do that, Alex?"

She chuckled. "Of course I did. What's happening now? It's hard to make out details from my view."

"Someone just pulled out a sat phone and is handing it to someone in an Al Hasib truck. Is that—" Hawk stopped, holding his breath as he strained to make out any more identifiable features.

"It's him, isn't it?" Alex said, breaking the silence. "Karif Fazil came to the exchange."

"Did I make it that obvious?"

"The only other person I could imagine you'd react like that to is dead, so I guess it was. Have you got him in your sights?"

"Sneaky bastard isn't letting me get a clean shot," Hawk said. "He's hiding behind the door, acting quite dodgy."

"Think he's nervous?"

"I know he's pissed. He's got one clenched fist, and his other hand is holding a gun."

"I'd guess that he just found out he doesn't have any money to buy that missile and realizes we've dried up another one of his money streams."

Hawk flinched as a gunshot erupted in the night

air, setting off a series of shots. Without hesitating, Fazil had raised his gun and fired a bullet at point-blank range into the head of Oberfelk's negotiator.

Guards from the two sides fanned back, taking cover behind their respective vehicles.

"I came prepared," Hawk said, studying the action through his scope. "But I didn't foresee anything like this happening. These fools are going to leave some serious carnage behind if anyone survives."

"You better make sure at least one of Oberfelk's men lives, that is if you don't want Fortner ripping you a new one."

"I got this," Hawk said. "I might even get a three-for-one if Fazil will move into view."

Hawk slung his rifle back over his shoulder and decided on a better course of action when considering his number one priority—eliminate the threat of an ICBM. Hustling down the tree, Hawk pulled the rocket-propelled grenade launcher off his back and took aim at the missile. The two sides continued their back and forth while Hawk prepared to take his shot.

Three, two, one . . .

He squeezed the trigger and braced himself for the kick that came from the launcher as the grenade went hurtling toward the missile.

The blast rocked the ground and set off a jarring explosion. Guards from both sides hit the jungle floor and looked up in awe as flames lapped high into the night sky. However, Fazil remained upright and took advantage of the situation, eliminating three of Oberfelk's men behind the cover of his truck.

Hawk scanned the area through his rifle's scope, cautiously optimistic the explosion hadn't outed him as a party crasher. Lying prone, he studied the field in front of him with the two sides continuing to exchange fire.

"Looks like you scored a direct hit there, Hawk," Alex said. "Congratulations."

"And bonus points for doing it anonymously," Hawk said. "I don't think they know I'm here yet."

"You do know how to announce yourself."

"Apparently not well enough, which is fine by me in this case."

Hawk slithered across the field toward the warm glow that lit most of the clearing. However, his heart sank when he watched the final two of Oberfelk's men crumple under a hail of bullets.

"There aren't any of Oberfelk's men to get since they're all dead. Now what?" Hawk asked as he froze.

"Take out Fazil," Alex answered. "I'm guessing you were already planning on that, but that's probably the only thing that will satisfy Fortner."

Hawk took aim at Fazil, subsequently eliminating the advantage of surprise. With all six bodies from

Oberfelk's men lying in plain view, Fazil would figure out soon enough that there was an intruder among them. Hawk watched Fazil and noticed where the shot had missed.

Just low and to the left.

Hawk adjusted his sight and continued his belly crawl as he sought a more favorable position to take his next shot.

Fazil glanced around the area, never moving from his protected place behind the truck door. He yelled something to his men, who rushed over to the vehicle. They piled into both trucks that had arrived with the caravan and roared out of the clearing.

"Damn it," Hawk said. "They're gone."

"Well, look on the bright side," Alex said, "it wasn't a complete failure of a mission. The weapon was crippled, and the country is safe for another night."

Hawk forced a laugh. "A lot of good that's going to do me when Fortner crawls all over me and blames me for failing to get the job done. And then I'll have to deal with Blunt."

"It's not the first time you've failed to accomplish all the mission objectives—and I doubt it'll be the last."

"Thanks for the vote of confidence."

"Just being honest," Alex said. "Black ops don't always go as smooth as you'd like them to. I knew that long before you signed up to stop the sale of this ICBM."

"I like it better when you're on site."

"Why's that?"

"You don't feel the need to be so honest when *we* fail."

She chuckled. "What's your next move?"

"See if I gather any info off these soldiers to bring back and let Fortner's Pentagon buddies analyze any devices for clues about Oberfelk's comings and goings."

"Well, you better make it quick because you're about to have company."

Hawk bolted upright and sprinted toward the dead bodies. "What do you mean?"

"I see three Humvees barreling toward your position. And I'd be willing to bet they aren't Fazil's men."

"That's all I need," Hawk said as he reached the first body. Hawk knelt beside it and felt the pockets until he retrieved a cell phone and small journal.

"Better make it snappy," Alex said. "I'm estimating you've got about fifteen seconds before they roll up on you."

Hawk checked another man quickly before finding nothing. As soon as Hawk saw the headlights flicker through the trees out of the corner of his eye, he hid a GPS tracker underneath the carriage of the truck before racing toward the edge of the woods. He crouched low in the shadows and watched the oncoming vehicles.

A team of men poured out of the trucks and cleaned up the scene. They collected as many bullet casings as they could find and scooped up all the bodies. A pair of men worked to put out the missile, which was still ablaze. After ten minutes, any random observer would've questioned if anyone had ever actually been in the clearing other than to chop down the trees and burn the undergrowth.

Hawk waited to give Alex an update until the men were finished and were driving away with the destroyed ICBM in tow.

He was about to raise Alex on his coms when he heard a twig snap in the jungle behind him. Hawk turned around slowly and strained to see into the darkness. He thought he saw something moving in the shadows but wasn't sure if his eyes were playing tricks on him. Refusing to move, Hawk remained planted in his spot. After ten minutes of relative silence, Hawk started walking in the direction of the noise.

As he went, Hawk reached into his pack and pulled out a pair of night vision goggles. He saw plenty of nocturnal wildlife mostly scurrying along the jungle floor with some occasional movement in the forest. But after slogging through the dense vegetation for a couple minutes, he stumbled upon something he didn't expect to see—a man stripped down to his t-shirt and boxers huddled in the fetal position next to a tree.

Hawk studied the man closely before speaking. Once his hands were in full view—and devoid of any weapons—Hawk addressed the man.

"Who are you?" Hawk demanded. "And what are you doing here?"

"I'm trying to survive," the man answered in heavily accented English while refusing to look up at Hawk.

"Survive? There are better ways to do it."

"Not if you don't want Karif Fazil to chop off your head."

"Did he leave you here?"

The man shook his head. "I escaped. He was going to kill me."

"What did you do?"

"I was supposed to secure the area. Apparently I failed. If I would have gone back to the truck, he would have killed me."

"How would you like to get revenge on your taskmaster?"

The man finally looked up at Hawk and scowled. "I do not wish him any harm. He took me in when no one else would."

"He took you in so he could use you," Hawk

said. "The fact that you understand that he would've killed you had you made it back to one of the vehicles proves you understand as much."

"Maybe I deserve it for not doing what Fazil told me to do."

Hawk chuckled. "You don't deserve it, as least not for that. My life depends on you not being able to even catch even a whiff of my scent when I'm on a mission like that. I was a ghost. You could've checked a thousand times, and I doubt you would've ever found me. It's not your fault."

"Fazil would have seen it another way."

"He would've killed you, yet here you are, still alive," Hawk said. "Don't you think that's for a reason?"

The man nodded. Hawk offered his hand to the man and pulled him to his feet.

"Why don't we go find out what that reason is," Hawk said. "What do you say?"

"Okay."

Hawk moved quickly and zip tied the man's hands behind his back. The man squirmed as he twisted away from Hawk. But he grabbed the man and forced him forward.

"What is this for?" the man asked, cutting his eyes to the side at his bound hands.

"I'm simply taking precautions," Hawk said. "For

all I know, you could be a plant left behind to kill me."

"Hiding in the bushes without a weapon?" the man asked. "You think that's how we're taught to ambush?"

"You can never be too careful. Now, come on, let's get moving. We've got a flight to catch."

Hawk nudged the man forward, and they continued along the path for several minutes. After a while, Hawk called Alex to update her on the situation.

"Where have you been?" she asked. "I was starting to worry about you once you left my screen and entered the jungle."

"I had to get out of there," Hawk said. "But on the positive side of things, I made a new friend."

"You made a new friend? What's his name?"

"To be determined, but he's one of Fazil's men. Found him hiding in the forest. He's not one of Oberfelk's guys, but, hopefully, he'll be a nice consolation prize for Fortner."

"Hustle back," she said. "We've got a lot of work to do."

CHAPTER 2

Washington, D.C.

THREE DAYS LATER, J.D. Blunt hobbled into the Pentagon meeting room and took a seat near the head of the table next to General Van Fortner. Hawk and Alex joined them before one lone straggler, an aide to President Noah Young, slipped into the room and shut the door before sitting down opposite Fortner.

"I appreciate everyone coming here today," he said, kicking off the meeting. "As you all are acutely aware, we are in some difficult times. And because of the work of the Firestorm team, things are a little less difficult and the world is a little safer."

"For now," Blunt grumbled.

"Exactly," Fortner said, pointing at Blunt. "For now. We dodged a bullet thanks to some great intel, but I shudder to think what might happen the next time Karif Fazil approaches an arms dealer about purchasing a long-range missile. He seems to be getting closer to making a breakthrough that would devastate this country."

"With all due respect, sir," Hawk said, "we're not going to let that happen."

"While I want to believe you, it's foolish to make such claims," Fortner said. "One wrong move and we all could be looking at a smoldering mushroom cloud over New York or Washington or Chicago or L.A."

"But at least we have a member of Al Hasib to extract information from," Alex said.

Fortner nodded. "Yes, at least we have that, though we haven't got much out of him yet. But we're working on it."

"I'm glad we caught the little bastard before the election," the aide chimed in. "If James Peterson were to win the presidency, there's no doubt the terrorist would receive a hero's welcome and be sent back to the Middle East with reparations for his time in U.S. custody."

Fortner sighed. "I know you're saying that in jest, but that might not be too from the truth. Part of the reason we need to work so hard to gather intelligence now is so we can force Fazil back into the open before the election. As much as the recent revelation about Peterson's alleged interaction with Al Hasib has damaged him in the polls, we all know how reliable polling numbers can be. All it takes is one story in the eleventh hour to change the minds of the American people."

"Well, let's give them a story that will make everyone have faith in Noah Young's leadership," Hawk said. "The head of Karif Fazil on a platter will do wonders for Young's popularity—as well as decimate Al Hasib."

"Agreed," Blunt said. "As strong of a tactician as Fazil is, his greatest strength is his charisma and ability to recruit able-bodied men to fight for him."

"So, what do you want us to do?" Hawk asked.

"I want to know what you need from me to make your job easier," Fortner said. "Access to tech, weapons, transportation, anything—you name it."

Hawk's eyes widened. "This might be a first in the history of the government."

Fortner flashed a quick smile. "Remember, you're not actually working for the government. That's why you're so successful at keeping terrorists at bay."

A polite, collective chuckle filled the room but quickly ended when Blunt groaned. He clutched his stomach and bent over slightly.

"Are you okay, J.D.?" Fortner asked.

"I'm fine," Blunt said. "Just a little stomach ache."

"Are you well enough to continue?" Fortner asked.

Blunt waved dismissively. "Go on, go on. We're all listening."

"The reason I ask about what you might need is because it's going to get increasingly more difficult to find Fazil now that his money supply has been cut off," Fortner said. "With most of his assets frozen, our ability to track him has decreased considerably."

"I didn't initiate that," Blunt said as he grimaced.

"I know you didn't," Fortner said. "Some stupid bureaucrat suggested it to Noah without running it by me first. We were able to learn more about his movements through tracking his money, even keeping tabs on his business associates and those loosely affiliated with Al Hasib through their fundraising efforts. But no longer."

"So what now?" Alex asked.

"From what we've been able to discern, Fazil has gone underground again," Fortner said.

"What if Al Hasib's funds were released?" Alex asked.

"That wouldn't matter," Fortner said. "He's going to lay low for a while, which might mean we don't have to worry about him for a period of time. But that also means we'll be in the dark about what he's planning—money or no money. He's not going to resurface until he's ready to act. And by then, it might be too late."

A knock at the door interrupted their discussion.

"Come in," Fortner said.

One of Fortner's aides poked his head inside the room. "Sorry to bother you, sir, but there's an urgent message for Senator Blunt."

Blunt furrowed his brow. "What is it?"

"A board member from Colton Industries just called on behalf of Thomas Colton's wife," the aide said. "He said that Mr. Colton has been kidnapped. And they think it's Al Hasib."

"Thank you," Fornter said, nodding at the aide to dismiss him.

"So much for Fazil staying underground and off the radar," Hawk said.

"He's a bull in a china shop now," Blunt said. "And we can put our plans on hold. The last thing we want is for Karif Fazil to somehow wrangle away some of Colton Industries' latest tech."

"Then let's get to it," Fortner said.

CHAPTER 3

Dallas, Texas

KARIF FAZIL GRINNED as he watched the files transfer to the portable hard drive he had connected to Thomas Colton's computer. To Fazil, fighting against the Americans always felt like entering battle with one hand tied behind his back. No matter how careful he was or how well he planned his attacks, they always seemed to have an advantage that mitigated any of his brilliant strategy. And that advantage seemed to come in the form of either technology or Brady Hawk. But Fazil had figured out a way to neutralize both advantages, and he was giddy with excitement while doing his best to contain his emotions.

"You know these documents are encrypted, right?" Colton said from the corner of the room as he fidgeted with the bindings around his wrists. "You won't be able to read them even though you have them."

"I know what *encrypted* means," Fazil said. "I doubt they will be too difficult for my Cal Tech-trained computer experts to crack. And if they are, I know where to find you."

"That's not my department," Colton said. "They don't let me near anything like that. I wouldn't know where to begin in finding you the right person to decrypt anything."

"Then let's just hope my men don't run into any problems."

Fazil crossed his arms and stepped back from the computer as he watched the file names populate the folder connected to his hard drive.

"You have a very dangerous son, Mr. Colton," Fazil said.

"Excuse me?" Colton said.

"I said, *you have a very dangerous son.*"

"Oh, you're talking about Brady Hawk," Colton said. "Well, come to find out, he's not exactly my son."

"And does he know that?"

"I think he was actually relieved when he found out."

"But he still cares for you, doesn't he?"

Colton shrugged. "Can't say for sure, though the only reason I ever see him these days is if he wants something from me."

"Is that how all kids are when they get older? They only come to see you if they need a handout?"

"I guess it's a universal trait among humans," Colton said, pausing for a moment before continuing the conversation. "Do you have any kids?"

Fazil wagged a finger at Colton. "Don't start with me, Mr. Colton. I know what you're trying to do. You're trying to connect with me and humanize yourself. But don't worry—I will never see any Americans as humans after what they did to my family. You will all pay at some point or another for the sins of your country's destructive military machine."

"That's not what I was trying to do. I was just—"

"Silence!" Fazil barked. "If I have a question, I will ask you and then you will speak. Is that understood?"

Colton nodded.

"Good," Fazil said. "Now that we're clear, it's time to go."

"Look, we can make a deal," Colton said. "It doesn't have to go down like this."

Fazil stormed across the room and backhanded Colton, drawing blood from the corner of his mouth. Stooping down to eye level, Fazil glared at Colton.

"What did I just say about speaking without being spoken to?"

Colton looked down.

Fazil grabbed Colton's face. "Look at me when I'm speaking to you."

Colton's gaze met Fazil's.

"Don't test me, Mr. Colton. You don't want to see what I'm capable of doing—not yet anyway."

Fazil strode back across the room to the computer and summoned his bird Jafar, which had been perched on the windowsill. Jafar lit on Fazil's shoulder and cooed.

Colton struggled with his bindings, his chair scraping against the floor as he tried to wrestle free. The noise resulted in a glance from Fazil. He turned and looked back at the screen.

"Don't bother with trying to escape," Fazil said. "It'll only make things worse for you."

Colton continued, refusing to look up at his captor.

With Jafar in tow, Fazil hustled across the room and delivered a vicious uppercut to Colton, connecting squarely with his chin. The blow knocked Colton backward. Fazil stood over his prisoner and studied him closely. Colton was out cold.

The computer beeped twice, signaling the task had been completed. Fazil hustled back to the terminal and snatched the thumb drive out of the USB slot. He stuffed the device into his pocket and returned to Colton, who still wasn't moving.

Fazil radioed for two of his men to retrieve Colton.

"I need him in the van," Fazil said. "We're not done with him yet."

CHAPTER 4

Dallas, Texas

UPON LANDING AT THE Dallas-Fort Worth airport, Hawk and Alex hustled to their rental car and drove to Dallas Executive Airport, which was where Thomas Colton kept his Gulfstream G650 jet. The latest report Hawk had received from Colton Industries was that one of the company security guards heard an Al Hasib agent mention something about stealing the boss's jet. And if that was true, Hawk understood the gravity of the situation.

Hawk was quite familiar with Colton's plane, which was a newer model year of the one Blunt often deployed for Firestorm missions. The Gulfstream G650 had one of the longest ranges of any executive jet on the market and could nearly fly Mach 1. If Fazil and his men got that jet in the air with Colton, they could disappear virtually anywhere in the world.

"What do you have in mind if Fazil has already taken Colton?" Alex asked.

"I'm hoping we don't have to deal with that, but I'm working on something."

"You know they're going to disable the GPS tracker."

Hawk nodded. "This isn't going to be easy." He slammed his fist on the steering wheel, fearing the inevitable.

"Calm down," she said. "We'll find him."

"I hate being a step behind Fazil."

"I'm sure the feeling is mutual."

"Well, he's got the upper hand right now."

"And look where that's gotten him."

Hawk shook his head. "He's still alive, isn't he?"

"He's getting desperate. And when you feel that way, you try to force the issue and make mistakes that end up costing you dearly. Fazil ought to know that from experience."

"But a brazen kidnapping like this on American soil demonstrates that he's reached a point where he feels like he has nothing to lose. And that scares the hell out of me."

"This is it for Fazil," Alex said. "And I think he knows it. This is his last-ditch attempt at doing anything. If he fails this time . . ."

She let her words hang, though Hawk wasn't in

agreement with Alex's conclusion. He wasn't convinced Fazil had reached the point where he would resign himself to failure if he didn't succeed on his next mission. Fazil was getting more desperate, but he still acted in a calculated manner. Kidnapping Colton was bold, but Hawk sensed there was purpose to it.

"My fear isn't that this is his last hurrah and that he's going for broke," Hawk said. "It's that he's going to put us in the kind of situation we can't win."

"That's the nature of the game, especially for someone who doesn't share your values. It's why we're in this whole battle in the first place."

"I know you're right, but it doesn't make it any easier to swallow."

Hawk entered the security checkpoint at Dallas Executive Airport and quickly parked before racing toward the Colton Industries hangar with Alex. The guard at the door sighed and shook his head slightly the moment he made eye contact with Hawk.

"They're gone," the man said.

"You let him take the plane?" Hawk asked before his mouth fell agape.

"I didn't have any choice. Mr. Colton made the request, though he didn't look like he made it willingly. But I doubt he had a choice."

"Did the terrorist have a gun?" Alex asked.

"I couldn't see one, but he held Mr. Colton tight

against him. I don't know what else he could've been trying to conceal."

"And they probably didn't file a flight plan, did they?" Hawk asked.

The man looked down at his desk and picked up a piece of paper before sliding it across the countertop to Hawk.

"Actually, they did file one."

Hawk looked at the final destination. "Port St. Lucia," he said with a chuckle. "I'm not buying that for a second."

"You and me both," the man said. "But if you want to know more about what's going on, I'd suggest you speak with Mr. Colton's wife, Gayle. I saw him call her before he left."

"Have the cops been by here yet?" Alex asked.

"Not yet, but they're on their way. They know something happened, but nobody at headquarters is telling them much of anything. I've been instructed to tell them it's all a big misunderstanding. But you guys aren't cops."

Hawk grinned. "Is Gayle in town?"

"She just got back two days ago from a trip somewhere in the Caribbean, and she hasn't been here since," the guard said. "And trust me, she doesn't set foot in airports. Just the mention of a commercial airport will result in her beginning a rant about how they are just a giant petri dish."

Hawk drummed on the counter before shaking the guard's hand.

"Thank you for your assistance. You've been most helpful."

"Sorry I couldn't tell you more, but you know everything I do now."

Alex nodded toward the door. "Let's get moving."

Once they got back to their car, Hawk fired up the engine and entered Colton's address into the GPS app on his phone.

"So do you have a hunch about anything yet?" Alex asked.

"I wish I had a better idea of what Fazil is thinking right now."

"You have many talents, Hawk, but unfortunately mind reading isn't one of them."

"I knew you were gonna say that before the words came out of your mouth," Hawk said.

"Are you trying to suggest that you can read minds?"

Hawk shook his head. "No, just that you're predictable in that way. You never miss a chance to needle me."

"Predictability, that's it," Alex said, getting excited. "That's the key to figuring out what Fazil is going to do next."

"A kidnapping of this nature is about as unpredictable as it gets for Fazil."

"No, it isn't," Alex said as she snapped. "Think about it. Whenever he makes a move like this, he's doing it for leverage or to gain a better position to unleash an attack on the U.S."

"So, which one is it?"

Alex sank in her seat and stared blankly out the window. "That I don't know. I'm not a mind reader."

"Exactly—and neither am I, which we're both finding out is most unfortunate."

Twenty minutes later, they pulled up to the gate of Thomas Colton's expansive estate. Sequestered among four other homes in a ritzy enclave that spanned nearly a hundred acres, it served as a respite from the seemingly endless wave of suburban neighborhoods with houses packed tightly next to each other.

"Guess everything really is bigger in Texas," Alex quipped.

"If you've got enough money," Hawk said.

He pressed the call button and waited. Moments later, Gayle's face appeared on the screen.

"Yes? May I help you?" she asked.

"Miss Gayle, it's me, Brady Hawk," he answered. "Can me and one of my associates have a few minutes of your time? It's about Thomas."

Even as the words came out of his mouth, they felt

strange. No matter how ready he was to move on from the news that Thomas Colton wasn't his father, Hawk still felt awkward calling the man anything other than *Dad*.

She dabbed at the corner of her eyes. "Okay, I guess I can speak with you for a few minutes."

The screen went black, and then the gates swung open.

"Did you two get along before?" Alex asked.

"Remember, I was supposedly the bastard child, so I wasn't exactly welcomed with open arms, especially when she found out that he was hiding my existence from her. Since the truth has come out, I'm just a reminder that her husband is a philanderer."

"Yet she won't give him up?"

"Take a look around," Hawk said. "She'd also have to give all of this up, not to mention that she lives for Dallas's high society. It's why she made him move from Houston."

"No comparison in the social scene?"

"That's what Colton told me once, though I'm only taking his word for it. I'm not exactly up on the high society happenings in Texas and where each city ranks accordingly. I hate that stuff."

"Me too."

"Yeah, about that. You might want to keep your opinions to yourself on such things. Gayle can be a great ally for us, or she can become a pretty formidable foe."

"I'll keep that in mind."

Hawk parked in the drive that circled a water fountain depicting a ring of mermaids all spitting water through their mouths into the center of the pool. Alex glanced at the pool and then at the three-story, Tudor-style house before taking in the rest of the grounds.

"Impressive, isn't it?" Hawk asked.

Alex nodded. "I knew I should've been a weapons manufacturer."

Hawk shook his head. "It'll get you a nice head, but it'll also get you kidnapped by maniacal terrorists. Sure you don't want to retract that last statement?"

Alex shrugged. "I've been kidnapped by those same kidnappers, except I'm not getting any of the benefits."

Hawk sighed. "Trust me, this life isn't what it's cracked up to be."

"Neither is trying to stop terrorists, but I'm dealing with it."

Hawk chuckled. "Alex, you love what you do. And I'm convinced this life would bore the hell out of you. Wearing high heels and sipping champagne while you talk about your latest show dog experience or trip to the Caribbean—that's not you."

"You're probably right, but I wouldn't mind giving it a try for a while."

Hawk knocked on the front door and waited for

Gayle. She opened it and welcomed them inside. She first hugged Hawk and held him tight.

Hawk looked at Alex, whose eyes widened.

"I don't know what this is," Hawk mouthed to her behind Gayle's back.

Then Gayle turned and hugged Alex.

"I'm so sorry, Miss Gayle," Alex said.

Gayle tried to hold back the stream of tears, but her attempts failed. The mascara streaked down her face as the waterworks flowed.

"They took him," Gayle said as she dabbed her eyes. "The bastards took Thomas. I don't know what I'm going to do."

"Did you speak with them?" Hawk asked.

She sniffled. "Let's sit down in the parlor."

Gayle led Hawk and Alex to a small sitting room and took a seat across from them. She paused a few moments to regain her composure before continuing.

"I wired them twenty million as Thomas instructed me this morning," she said. "I know they were making him tell me to do it."

Alex whistled. "Twenty million. My god."

"Yeah, that's about the same response I had," Gayle said, "though I threw in a few choice words as well. But that's not all."

"They want more?" Hawk asked.

"Twenty million more," she said.

"And you're supposed to wire it to them when?" Hawk asked.

"Actually, I'm not supposed to wire this amount," Gayle said. "They want this portion in cash."

"Cash? How do they think you're going to get it to them?"

"They don't want me to give it to them—they want you to do it."

Hawk withdrew and scowled. "Me? They expect me to do it?"

"Apparently you're their delivery boy of choice, but that doesn't mean I'm not going with you."

"And where am I going?" Hawk asked.

"Morocco, I think."

"I don't like how this sounds."

"But that's not all the details," Gayle said. "Aside from the twenty million in cash, you're supposed to call a number they gave me once you reach Moroccan airspace, and they will tell you what airport to land at."

"Sneaky bastards. They're really intent on making sure I don't bring the cavalry with me."

"No way you're going without me," Gayle said.

"Or me either," Alex added.

"Of course you are," Hawk said. "I doubt I could stop either one of you, even if I tried."

CHAPTER 5

Washington, D.C.

NOAH YOUNG WASN'T READY to make his move into the White House permanent just yet, but he felt like a man with the game in hand and his opponent was helpless to stop him. That was the kind of advantage he was happy to take after outing his opponent's son as a conspirator in allowing a terrorist into the country to detonate a suitcase nuke in the middle of New York City. The election seemed to be all but a foregone conclusion. However, Young didn't carry that confidence into public, preaching that the American people needed to go out and vote. He surprised himself with the amount of passion he was able to muster in hammering home that campaign message.

An aide dropped off a copy of the latest polling reports and lingered while Young read them.

"Looking good," Young said. "I think this is

what we were all hoping to see."

"Yes, sir," the aide replied. "Just over a week to go, and everything is pointing toward you being chosen by the American people."

Young thanked the man and watched him slip out of the door. With lunch fast approaching, Young interlocked his fingers behind his head and leaned back, basking in the feeling of a looming triumph. There was still plenty of work to be done to secure the presidency, but he could almost taste it.

If I'm sitting in this chair in two weeks, it'll be because I earned it, not because I hitched my horse to Conrad Daniels, God rest his soul.

In a moment of self-honesty, Young admitted a more brutal truth lurked beneath the surface of his brash statement. Reality was hidden beneath an avalanche of intangibles that served as a more-constant reminder of his good fortune rather than his shrewd political posturing. Losing to a candidate who had family connections to what would've been the deadliest terrorist attack on American soil, perhaps the deadliest attack of any kind in the country's history, would be a task of nearly insurmountable odds. This fact was even more apparent given that Young didn't have any skeletons in his closet that could compete with the albatross swinging from James Peterson's neck.

Right place, right time.

That was the truth when Young looked objectively at all the facts and the way everything had played out. He received the nod for vice president when Conrad Daniels went looking for a running mate who could win a few extra votes as opposed to losing them. Young possessed dashing good looks—dark complexion, strong jaw line, sparkling blue eyes, a megawatt smile, and a smooth voice that commanded attention—and a political record that was more centrist than activist. And when pressed about the matter in an exploratory interview with Daniels's aides, Young admitted he had no aspirations of ever becoming president. All those factors combined to make him the perfect vice presidential candidate.

But that seemed like ages ago in political time.

Young had changed along with his aspirations. The waters of discontent went from stirred to thrashing waves. Over the final six months of Daniels's life, Young had grown ill thinking about the possibility of remaining as the president's "yes man" for another term. Even though he saw the power he could wield from his position to keep Daniels in check and mitigate any policy missteps regarding terrorism in the Middle East, Young yearned to trade his behind-the-scenes role for a more prominent one. Perhaps playing second fiddle awakened a desire he never realized he had. Whatever the reason for his newfound drive to become president, Young felt invigorated and hopeful about the future of the country.

As Young was pondering the coming months and what he would do in his first hundred days in office, his cell phone rang with a number he didn't recognize. He'd adopted a policy of ignoring calls from numbers he didn't have entered into his contact list. With the swipe of his finger, he sent the caller straight to voicemail. His secretary could transcribe the message for him later. Seconds later, a text message appeared on the phone's screen:

check under your desk

Young furrowed his brow and wondered who the mystery caller was. Nevertheless, he groped beneath his desk, feeling around until he came upon a smooth piece of paper. He knelt down and looked at the object: a white envelope, taped tightly to the bottom of the center drawer.

What's this?

He tore open the envelope and dug out a letter that had been folded several times. Fold by fold, Young slowly returned the paper to its original size before reading it.

Questions abound. The American people deserve to know the truth about what happened that day.

Beneath it was a website address along with a login code. Young pecked the address into the appropriate location at the top of his web browser. Moments later, a black screen appeared with a white box in the center, presumably for the code. After keying in the password, Young waited for the website to materialize. Once the site loaded, the same words written on the note were also posted at the top of the page. In the center was a video still obscured only by a universal play symbol.

Young furrowed his brow and dragged his mouse on top of the image before clicking. A split second later, the video went full screen and started to play.

The image appeared shaky and looked to be shot from the viewpoint of someone running through the woods. The image grew steadier as the person behind the camera found a place to rest and presumably hide. However, the shot swept across a stretch of woods. Almost immediately, Young recognized the location and cringed. He knew what he was about to see.

Depicted on camera was Young along with Brady Hawk talking with a bedraggled Conrad Daniels. Thirty seconds later, Daniels was shown slitting his wrist and bleeding out.

Anybody who watched the images on the screen would have a mountain of questions, given that the official narrative of Conrad Daniels's death was that of a heart attack. But Daniels obviously died another way. So, why lie about it? Why keep the truth from the American people? What drove Daniels to do this? Did he have mental health issues? Was he under the influence of drugs? Was he coerced? Threatened? And why did the vice president and some other man just let it happen without calling for help in a reasonable amount of time?

That was just the beginning of the questions the media and public would be asking if they watched the final minutes of Conrad Daniels's life. A video like this would certainly erode the people's trust in him along with his chances of winning the presidency.

Young's phone buzzed, alerting him to another text message from the mysterious caller.

That wasn't natural causes from a heart attack. Ready to talk?

Young wasn't ready to talk because the American people weren't ready to hear the truth, though he doubted they ever would be. Their attempts to sweep Daniels's death under the rug had suddenly become an October surprise in December—and one of his own making.

Young only wanted to make the video—and the person behind it—simply go away.

CHAPTER 6

HAWK ONLY HAD TO WAIT six hours for J.D. Blunt to show up at the Dallas Executive Airport with his jet prepped for the long flight to Morocco. During that time, Hawk and Alex tried to comfort Gayle by exuding confidence in their ability to get her husband back from Al Hasib. Hawk also discussed with Alex the best way to handle any forthcoming negotiations with the terrorists. Without knowing the full extent of their demands, they decided such an exercise was futile, especially since the possibilities seemed too numerous to reach any consensus approach.

When Blunt's plane landed, he lumbered down the stairs, using his cane to steady himself. He grimaced with each step and offered a weak attempt at a wave once he reached the ground.

"Does he look all right to you?" Alex asked.

Hawk shook his head. "I know this business of fighting Al Hasib has taken a toll on everyone, but he seems to be taking it the hardest."

"But he looks like someone who's endured more than just a stressful period of life," she said. "He looks like he's suffering."

"Perhaps, but he always seems to labor beneath the burden of responsibility."

"But don't we all?"

"Yes, but not as much as Blunt does."

Hawk and Alex walked forward to meet Blunt, exchanging handshakes and congenial hugs. They led him over to Gayle, who went straight for a long embrace.

"Please get him back for me," Gayle said, refusing to let go.

Blunt waited for a moment before withdrawing. "We'll do our best to bring him home."

She shook her head. "And I'll be right there with you."

"But I don't think—"

"I'm coming too, J.D., whether you like it or not. This is my Tommy we're talking about."

Blunt took a deep breath and shrugged. "Feel free to tag along, but just know that we can't guarantee your safety. Everyone here has a part in this mission and can't be bogged down by having to guard you."

"I understand and accept full responsibility for myself."

"In that case, let's go get your husband," Blunt said, gesturing toward the plane.

They all grabbed their luggage, piled into Blunt's jet, and then hurried to prepare for takeoff.

Once they were in the air, Blunt sat next to Hawk and Alex to discuss how they would handle the ransom and exchange.

"Do you have the money?" Blunt asked.

Hawk shot a glance toward the back of the plane where Gayle sat with four large suitcases. "She said she would pay any amount she could to get her husband back. And I think she really meant that."

"Well, that's one part of the equation," Blunt said. "But we need to be able to track that money. The fact that Al Hasib already wrested twenty million from the Coltons is a travesty in and of itself, but now they're going to double that? We're going to have to be perpetually on high alert until we're able to shut down that account."

"We've got some people working on tracing the money," Alex said. "We'll figure out a way to refuse them access to it."

"That's why twenty million in cases creates a different kind of issue."

"We got a list of the serial numbers from a random sampling of the money," Alex said. "They won't be able to deposit that without red flags being raised."

"That's what I'm afraid of," Blunt said. "What if they decide to deal in cash now? We're really shooting ourselves in the foot with this approach, just like I told the folks at the Pentagon."

"I think we're all in agreement on that," Hawk said, "but there's not a lot we can do about it now. This is the hand we've been dealt, so we just have to figure out a way to win without any aces up our sleeves."

"It's hard to win when you don't know what game you're playing," Blunt said.

"At its core, this is a mind game," Alex said. "Karif Fazil knew Gayle would pay and had the connections to get Hawk to deliver the money."

"But why Hawk?" Blunt asked. "Unless of course, it's a set up."

"Fazil wouldn't do that," Hawk said. "He's got too much pride. If he wanted to kill me, he had plenty of chances in the past. I think he's more focused on wanting me to see him triumph than he is on simply killing me. In my conversations with him and based on what we know from intel reports, Fazil's ire is directed at the U.S. government and our military for what happened to his family. He's not some idealistic jihadist as he wants the world to believe—he's simply out for revenge."

"You're right, Hawk," Blunt said. "I doubt he's doing this so he can put you in his sights and shake you. This might not be the kind of set up to kill you; however, he's definitely setting you up for something. And whatever it is, it won't be good."

"I'll figure out something," Hawk said.

"Your life depends on it this time—as does Colton's."

Hawk nodded as he closed his eyes.

What are you up to, Karif Fazil?

Hawk fell asleep, contemplating the question that would surely haunt him in his dreams.

* * *

HAWK AWOKE WITH A NUDGE from Alex. He rubbed his eyes and shielded them from the sunshine streaming through the window.

"What's going on?" he asked.

"Welcome back, sunshine," Alex said. "I wasn't sure if you were ever going to emerge from your beauty sleep. For a while I thought we were gonna have to find a princess to kiss you."

"I was sleeping that hard?"

"We went through multiple time zones along with three rough patches of turbulence, one of which rattled loose a cupboard door in the kitchen and resulted in a pile of dishes sliding across the cabin floor."

"And I didn't wake up?" Hawk asked.

"You didn't even stir," Alex said. "I was quite impressed."

"Guess I was due for a long sleep."

"You're still not as sound of a sleeper as Gayle over there," Blunt said, pointing with his eyes. "She fell asleep before you did—and she's still out."

"Are you sure you weren't pumping some aerosol version of Ambien through the ventilation system?'"" Hawk asked.

Blunt smiled and patted Hawk on his shoulder. "Wake up quickly because it's time to get to work."

"Where are we?"

"In Moroccan air space," Alex said. "Time to make the call."

She handed Hawk the phone as he sat up straight. He rubbed his eyes once more and took a swig from the bottled water situated in his seat's cup holder.

"Here it goes," he said.

He pushed the send button and waited for a response. After three rings, a man answered the call.

"Is this Mr. Hawk?" the man asked.

"It is."

"Take down the following coordinates."

The man proceeded to list a string of numbers, which Hawk scratched down onto a scrap piece of paper.

"Give those coordinates to your pilot," the man. "That should get you to the Marrakesh Airport. Once you arrive, taxi to hangar number thirty-seven. Remain in the plane until we call you. A refueling tanker will refill your tanks and prepare you for the next leg of your journey. Understand?"

"Roger that," Hawk said before he hung up.

He tossed the phone back to Alex before standing and striding toward the cockpit. He knocked on the door and handed the coordinates to the co-pilot.

"Change of plans, men," Hawk said. "We need you guys to put this bird down in Marrakesh. You have the numbers in case you need them."

The two men nodded and looked at Hawk.

"We'll be there in less than ten minutes," the co-pilot said.

Hawk returned to his seat and reported the status back to the rest of the passengers.

"You ready for this?" Alex asked.

"We're about to find out, aren't we?"

Once the plane touched down, the pilots maneuvered the jet to the assigned hangar and waited. As promised, a tanker rushed up next to the plane and started the refueling process.

"Think this is going to be some kind of game where Fazil sends us all over the world?" Alex asked.

"It already is."

Gayle was wide awake at this point and on edge. She dipped into her purse and pulled out a flask, throwing back a few shots before slipping it back inside. She wiped her mouth with the back of her hand

and leaned forward in her seat, straining to see out the window.

"What's going to happen next?" she asked.

"They'll let us know what to do," Hawk said. "Just try to relax."

"I just want Tommy home," she said, tears welling in her eyes. "I want this whole thing to be over with."

"You're in good hands, Mrs. Colton," Alex said. "Don't worry."

Gayle's phone rang, and she answered it immediately.

"Hello," she said.

"Give the phone to Brady Hawk," a man on the end said loud enough that they could all hear it.

She complied.

"What's next?" Hawk asked.

"Take the money, and place it on the cart being delivered in front of the door of your plane," the man said. "Then drive the cart east along the edge of the tarmac until you reach a giant white x. Once you reach there, open the suitcases to show us the money. Once we see the money, we'll signal for you to step away from the cart and come toward our plane. At that time, we'll release Mr. Colton."

"Sounds easy enough."

"One more thing, Mr. Hawk."

"What's that?"

"No weapons. We're watching you, and if we see you so much as pretend like you're going to draw your gun, you'll have a bullet in your head and be dead before you hit the ground. Understand?"

"I understand," Hawk said, "but also understand this: Gayle Colton is coming with me. She's not going to wait to see her husband."

There was a brief pause and some murmuring.

"We will allow it," the man said before he hung up.

Hawk handed the phone back to Gayle and explained the protocol as he understood it. Once the stairs were lowered, Hawk helped Gayle down them. He began loading the suitcases of cash onto the baggage cart Al Hasib dropped off nearby, while Blunt and Alex remained in the back of the plane and out of sight. If Al Hasib happened to notice the other Firestorm team members, Hawk warned that it could set off a gunfight.

After he finished loading the vehicle, Hawk flashed a quick salute to the pilots and wheeled the cart in the direction given to him by the Al Hasib agent. With each hangar situated about 300 meters apart, Hawk had some time for a few last-minute words with Gayle.

"It's going to be over in just a few minutes,"

Hawk said, placing his hand on top of Gayle's.

She looked at him and forced a smile.

"You know, I always resented you and what you stood for, Brady. You were the constant reminder of Tommy's indiscretions, his moral failings. Every time I saw you, I wanted to punch you and then punch Tommy. And even after I found out that you weren't the result of one of his affairs, I couldn't see you as anything else. But I don't feel that way any more."

Hawk smiled and squeezed her hands.

"You're a good woman, Gayle, especially for sticking with Thomas. I can't imagine he'd be an easy man to be married to."

"No, he's not. But he's mine, and I still love him, despite all his faults."

"Nobody's perfect, but I hope he's become more tame in his old age."

She nodded. "He has. We dealt with the past and moved on. It wasn't easy, but it's helped me realize how much I appreciate him."

"For what it's worth, he always treated me well when I was younger. And as much as he's done some irksome things lately, I would certainly never let him twist in the wind, especially at the hands of Al Hasib."

"Thank you," she said. "I know I've been hysterical, but I'm glad this is almost over."

Hawk decided to let Gayle live in her dream

world. He suspected they were only getting started.

"Looks like we've almost arrived at our destination," she said, pointing to the freshly painted white x on the tarmac.

Hawk slowed the cart to a halt and then climbed out. He glanced around and noticed Colton's plane lurking in the shadows of the next hangar.

"Do you see your husband's plane in the hangar over there?" Hawk asked.

She craned her neck to see into the unlit building. "Are you sure? It's so dark."

"I'm sure. I'm going to hold the money up in that direction."

Hawk proceeded to open the cases and turn toward the hangar. He hoisted stacks of cash and pointed inside. One by one, he went through the four suitcases in the same manner until he saw some men emerge from around the corner of the hangar. They motioned for Hawk and Gayle to walk toward them, just as had been explained on the earlier call.

Hawk and Gayle walked about a hundred meters, Gayle clutching Hawk's arm and staying close. Another cart toting a trio of guards raced out to the location where Hawk had left the suitcases. Hawk glanced over his shoulder at the men before returning his gaze forward. The other men near the hangar gestured for Hawk and Gayle to stop.

"What do you suppose is the problem?" she asked.

Hawk looked behind him at the guards transferring the suitcases from one cart to the other.

"You don't think the bank shorted you any money, do you?" he asked.

"No, of course not. I told them that every dime had better be there. Do you think that's what's going on?"

Hawk shrugged. "I'm not sure, but whatever it is, I don't like it."

He surveyed the scene cautiously, feeling naked without a weapon. If Karif Fazil wanted Hawk eliminated, this would be the prime moment. And while Hawk held firm to his belief that Fazil wanted to first gloat with a victory on U.S. soil, the assassin wondered if he'd been overconfident in assessing the psyche of Al Hasib's leader.

Hawk and Gayle remained frozen as they waited for the next actionable moment. A half a minute later, Thomas Colton staggered out of the shadows and walked toward them. He appeared as if he'd undergone a severe interrogation or two. Colton wove back and forth as he moved toward them, his attempts at moving in a straight line resulting in a wobbly path. Gayle shortened the distance by ignoring the orders to stay put and raced toward him.

Hawk watched as one of the guards raised his weapon.

Please, don't shoot.

The guard relented when the baggage cart rolled to a stop in front of his line of sight. A pair of guards jumped in the vehicle and zoomed toward Blunt's plane. Everything happened so fast, but Hawk saw the situation unfolding as if it were in slow motion.

He hustled over to Gayle, who tried to hold up Colton on her own. Neither one of them were doing well, Colton unable to stand and Gayle unleashing a stream of tears.

"I need your phone," Hawk said to Gayle.

She sniffled and dried her eyes before digging into her purse for her cell. After a brief search, she held it up just as it began to buzz.

"Well, what do you know?" she said, blissfully unaware of what was happening.

Hawk took the phone and answered it.

"This wasn't part of the deal," Hawk said as he answered.

Karif Fazil was on the other line. "I think you are getting everything that you were promised. Sorry that it doesn't meet your expectations."

Hawk watched as the guards stormed Blunt's plane. Seconds later, the engines began to whine in a high-pitched sound until they were roaring.

"My expectations were that we would make an exchange—Thomas Colton for the cash."

"If there is one thing I have learned in life, it is that things do not always go as you expect them to, Mr. Hawk. So, now that I have your attention, we need to talk. I'll be in touch soon."

Hawk narrowed his eyes as he watched Blunt's plane zoom down the runway, gaining speed before the jet lurched skyward.

CHAPTER 7

Zagros Mountains, Iraq

KARIF FAZIL HELD HIS PALM flat so Jafar could peck at the spread of breadcrumbs. Fazil's pet bird bobbed its head up and down, scarfing down every piece until Fazil's hand was clean, devoid of even a scant morsel. Against the far wall in the Al Hasib hideout, Fazil watched the security camera footage of Hawk holding a phone as he stood helpless in front of a hangar at the Marrakesh airport.

"What do you think, Jafar? Should we give him a call back?" Fazil asked aloud. "I would be willing to bet that the suspense is killing him."

Jafar fluttered away to his perch across the room.

With a smug grin, Fazil dialed the phone number Hawk had just called from. Fazil watched as Hawk furrowed his brow while studying the screen.

"This is Hawk," he said as he answered.

"Brady Hawk, it is truly wonderful to hear your voice again," Fazil said.

"I'm not in the mood for games."

"What a shame," Fazil said. "You're so good at them."

"Like the one I schooled you in when you were in New York?"

Fazil moaned and then continued. "As much as I hate that you foiled my brilliant plan, I have to give credit where credit is due. You figured out a way to thwart my scheme, and it was quite an ingenious idea at that. I thought I had everything covered, but I learned a valuable lesson that day: Never underestimate the power of a good partner. It is essential to success."

"So you kidnapped my partner to even the playing field?"

"That is one way to look at it, but I'm viewing this situation in a different light."

"How so? This looks like a pretty simple hostage situation to me."

"Actually, I'm putting into practice what I learned. After much thought and reflection on what went wrong in New York, I realized that my efforts were not supported with a good partner, merely good soldiers. There is a difference I now understand."

"If you're going where I think you're going with

this, you can stop right now and dream on. It's never gonna happen."

"Do not be so hasty to reject my offer," Fazil said. "I have spent considerable time pondering what might happen if we joined forces instead of fighting against one another."

"It'll be a cold day in Hell before I ever help you do anything."

"I would caution you, Mr. Hawk, against making such blanket statements, especially when the person you love the most and the man you look to as a father figure are both being held captive by Al Hasib forces."

"If you lay a hand on her, I swear I'll—"

"You are also not in a position to make threats. In American parlance, I believe the phrase is I hold all the cards."

"I don't care what cards you're holding, you can shove up them up your ass. I won't be manipulated to do your bidding. The two prisoners you temporarily hold will prove to be your downfall. It was a bold move, Karif, but one you will regret for eternity in Hell."

Fazil laughed heartily. "Such boldness and courage and passion. It's why we'll make a great team."

"Perhaps there is a language barrier between us. So let me clear this up for you once and for all: I will never partner with you."

Fazil shook his head and chuckled. "Oh, but I

think you will. You are full of the American bravado, but it will not get you far in a negotiation. And that's what we are doing here."

"A negotiation? This sounds more like you trying to give me an order."

"Call it whatever you wish, but you will do what I ask."

"I swear you are either deaf or stupid."

"I could say the same about you," Fazil said. "Perhaps you fail to understand the gravity of the situation facing Alex once she arrives. My men are—how can I put this delicately—rather deprived in certain areas of their lives. Giving themselves over to a cause as great as the jihad waged by Al Hasib means certain pleasures must be sacrificed. But if you continue to refuse my invitation to work for me on this upcoming mission, I would not hesitate to give them a reprieve, if you understand what I mean."

"I clearly understand what you mean, and I can promise you that I will scatter your ashes to the four winds after this is all over, regardless of what happens with Alex and J.D. while they're in your custody."

"I can assure you that they'll be well taken care of," Fazil said. "And based on your answer, I'm glad that you have come around to see things my way and have chosen to embark on this mission."

"And what exactly is this mission?"

"I want you to help me kill Noah Young."

Hawk laughed. "You are insane, aren't you? Do you honestly believe I'm going to kill the president for you?"

"Not *kill* the president. *Help* me kill the president."

"This won't end well, even if you succeed."

"Perhaps not, but I'm betting it will end better than my last attempts at seeking revenge on U.S. soil, if for any reason other than you won't be there to stop me this time."

"You know I can't do this."

"Can not or will not? There is a considerable difference. From what I can see, you look completely healthy and capable of doing what I need to be done."

"And what do you hope that I'll be able to do for you?"

"I will send you the information you need in due time. Until we speak again," Fazil said.

He hung up and watched the feed as Hawk seethed, storming around the hangar, looking as if he wanted to hit something. Fazil couldn't help but laugh when he saw Hawk slam him fist into the side panels of one of the planes parked just inside.

"See Jafar," Fazil said looking across the room toward his bird, "I told you Mr. Hawk would eventually come around."

CHAPTER 8

Washington, D.C.

NOAH YOUNG WOULD'VE PREFERRED to meet with the blackmailer at Camp David or any other site along the campaign trail. Potentially explosive news surrounding such a meeting could be kept under wraps much easier away from 1600 Pennsylvania Avenue. But with the election nearing and his campaign advisors recommending Young stay in Washington to tend to business and present a picture of experience and strength from the White House, he complied.

The procedure for sneaking the man into the White House was rather simple. He posed as an aide for one of a handful of senators Young was scheduled to meet with that morning. Such protocol wasn't out of the norm as aides sat in on meetings that weren't sensitive in nature oftentimes. No one even raised an eyebrow or asked who the man was as he followed closely behind Sen. Milton Delaney.

"I appreciate this, Milt," Young said as Delaney entered the room with his aide, who went by the alias of John Smith.

"I'm more than happy to help," Delaney said, "and more than happy to get your support on the immigration bill I'll be submitting in January."

"Of course," Young said. "Whatever you want."

Delaney smiled and shook Young's hand before slipping back down the hallway. If anyone noticed Delaney had lost his companion, word never got back to Young that afternoon.

"Please have a seat," Young said, gesturing toward an open chair across from him.

Both men sat down. Young leaned forward and asked his guest if he wanted coffee or water. He declined and suggested they get straight to business.

"I must begin by saying that this is highly unusual," Young said. "Such demands often land you in prison or under surveillance by the Secret Service."

"In that case, I appreciate you keeping quiet about this meeting, if anything for your own sake. As I warned before, I have plenty of stopgap measures in place should this not play out to my liking."

"All right then. Let me see if I can address your concerns. But first, I must know your name."

"I know this may be irritating to you, but I'm not

ready to give up my identity," the man said. "You know me as John Smith, which is about as much as I want to say about it. It's for my own protection—and possibly yours too, you know, plausible deniability and the like."

Young sighed and shook his head. "I don't like this. I try to be transparent with my governing as well as who I'm meeting with."

"Then maybe you should've been transparent with the American people in the first place about the real reason why President Daniels is dead."

"The truth is complicated," Young said.

"Doesn't look that complicated to me," Smith shot back. "Daniels looked angry and vindictive as he committed suicide. Something had clearly gone wrong."

"He snapped, plain and simple. But if I had gone out and told the American people that Daniels committed suicide because he flipped out, no one would've believed me. Politicians and pundits would've accused me of trying to make some power play, which couldn't be further from the truth."

"But you see, that's the problem, Mr. President. We're all further away from the truth because of the lies foisted upon the American public in the first place. If you'd just come out in the first place and—"

"I don't know what axe you have to grind, much

less where you got a copy of that video, but let me assure you that there was no foul play involved. I think deep down you need to ask yourself if our country is better off for seeing one of its strongest leaders take his own life? Do you feel like they have some right to see it? Because rest assured, it will steal any dignity Conrad Daniels had regarding the end of his life. He went out on his terms, and I can assure that he had no intentions of anyone else witnessing his final act on this planet."

Smith shifted in his chair. "I haven't decided whether I even have the right to make the decision for people regarding the contents of the video. But what I do know is that the American people are owed the truth, which is something only you can give them. I can go to the press with this footage, and it'll stir up plenty of trouble for you right before the election. But that's not how I want this to play out. I simply want you to set the record straight."

"I'll think about it," Young said as he leaned back in his chair.

"No, don't think about it—do it. You have a big rally in two days at the Capital One Arena downtown. I can't think of a better opportunity for you to cease with this charade and tell America what really happened that day and why. And who knows, maybe it'll even boost your poll numbers."

"I appreciate the courtesy of you coming to me first, though I must admit I don't like the way you've cast veiled threats on this office if I don't do exactly as you say. Once I take the time to examine all sides of this issue, I'll make a decision and act accordingly."

"That's not how this goes, Mr. President. You're going to tell everyone what happened at the rally or else I'm going to put that video on the Internet. It'll go viral, and your political career just might be finished. But if you're willing to chance it, that's your decision. But I will be watching."

Young glared at Smith. "You better be watching your back, too."

"Speaking of veiled threats," Smith said as he stood. "Killing me isn't going to kill this footage, just so you know. Killing me will only make things worse for you, but you do what you need to do."

"I will," Young said. "Now, if you'll excuse me, I need to get back to the business of governing this country."

Smith exited the room without even glancing back at Young. With stealthy movements, Smith eased the door shut behind him. A half a minute later, a knock at the door startled Young, shaking him out of his trance. He was still seething over Smith's demands when the voice outside interrupted him.

"Mr. President, I have some paperwork for you

to look at now that your meeting is over," one of Young's aides said.

"Come in," Young said.

The aide dropped a stack of documents on the desk before stopping and staring at the president.

"Is everything all right, Mr. President?"

Young nodded slowly. "Everything is fine."

"Well, you just seem kind of down. Is everything okay? Who was that last guy you met with? I didn't recognize him nor was his name on the schedule today since I know what all of them look like."

"That's none of your concern. But everything is fine now. Just stressed about the upcoming election, that's all."

"Well, sir, with all due respect, you don't really have much to worry about. I saw the latest polls this afternoon, and you've built pretty much an insurmountable lead with less than a week to go."

"Fickle are the November winds," Young said.

"Good thing this election is being held in December."

Young forced a smile. "I'll take a look at these and get back with you on them tomorrow."

"No problem, sir," the aide said. "I won't take up any more of your time, sir. I'll see you tomorrow afternoon then."

Left alone to ponder what he should do, Young

felt his stomach churn. He knew the decision to hide the truth from the American people could come back to haunt him; he just hoped that if it ever did, it would've been years later, unable to do any damage to Daniels's reputation and deliver more pain for his family. Young needed to squelch this story before it took on a life of its own. But was a public confession the best way to do that? Young wasn't so sure.

CHAPTER 9

HAWK STRODE THROUGH a Pentagon hallway and made his way to the conference room, where General Van Fortner sat waiting. Once Hawk locked eyes with Fortner, the general's face dropped. He looked at the floor and shook his head.

"I'm so sorry, Hawk," Fortner said. "I don't know how we didn't anticipate this."

"Fazil surprised us all with his bait and switch maneuver," Hawk said. "Given the fact that we'd just frozen all of Al Hasib's assets, why would we have suspected anything more? We knew they were desperate for cash, and we couldn't see past that. Tactically, I have to tip my hat to Fazil on this move. It wasn't just bold; it was also a blindside."

"Now it's time for us to return the favor."

"I like the sound of that, but we can't forget that

Fazil has two of our best," Hawk said. "We can't put them in more danger than they're already in—and any attempts at stringing Fazil along is going to result in that."

"I'm assuming Fazil has some conditions for returning Alex and J.D."

Hawk nodded, unsure if he wanted to reveal the demands. Staring blankly at the wall for a few seconds, he struggled with what to say next.

"Hawk, what is it? What does he want you to do?"

Hawk didn't flinch, maintaining his distant gaze.

"Help me out here," Fortner said. "What does Fazil want you to do?"

"He wants me to help him kill the president," Hawk said, his voice stripped of any inflection or emotion. "He wants Noah Young dead."

"Bastard," Fortner said as he slammed his fist on the table. "That's a situation that won't be easy to escape."

"Not without some serious collateral damage. And I don't think either one of us are willing to let that happen, are we?"

"Not a chance. I'd send a team of Rangers in to rescue Alex and J.D.—if I only knew where they were."

Hawk sighed. "That'd only make Fazil more determined. I know it might not seem possible now, but

I think he'd turn into an even more dangerous foe if we did that to him."

"We need put him down before this turns into Osama bin Laden all over again."

"Agreed," Hawk said, nodding resolutely. "We've had our chances, but every time we put him in the crosshairs, pulling the trigger would usually mean more senseless tragedy. So far, we've been able to stave that off by thwarting his attacks. But at some point, he's going to get the better of us if we don't take him out once and for all."

"Think you can find out where he is?"

"It's possible, but without Alex, I don't know that I'll be able to successfully pull it off."

"I'd send some of my best Rangers with you. You'd have an elite team around you to assist in the operation."

"Then I guess all I have to do is find out where they are, which is easier said than done."

"You said you might have a way. At this point, it's all we've got."

Hawk nodded. "Let me try my contacts and see what I come up with. I'll get back with you once I hear something."

After leaving the Pentagon, Hawk returned to one of Blunt's secret apartments downtown. Blunt had a few numbers stuck in his head from his time in

Iraq, though he wasn't sure any of them would lead to the person he needed to talk to: Kejal.

Kejal's uncle, Jaziri, had been a great asset for the Seals over the years on secret missions in Iraq. Hawk had met the elderly man just once while with the Seals, but the bond they forged was a lasting one. When Hawk went on one of his first missions with Firestorm, he leaned heavily on Jaziri to gain a tactical position on an alleged Al Hasib hideout. Jaziri's willingness to assist Hawk cost the old man his life, according to his nephew Kejal. Out of desire for revenge, Kejal joined Al Hasib with the intention of sabotaging future operations and getting even with the soldier who killed his uncle. Without Kejal's help escaping a few weeks earlier from an Al Hasib prison, Hawk might still be stuck in the desert while New York dealt with a nuclear fallout. The fact that the world was a much better place because of Kejal wasn't something Hawk would ever forget.

But Hawk needed Kejal's help again.

Dialing an old number Hawk recalled from his memory bank, he hoped for a friendly voice on the other end of the line.

"*Alo*," said the voice of what sounded like a middle-aged woman to Hawk.

Hawk spoke in Arabic. "I am trying to reach Kejal. Could you help me get in contact with him?"

"Who is this?"

"I am a friend of Jaziri's. And I also know Kejal."

"If you were a friend of Jaziri, you would know that he is dead."

"I was a friend of Jaziri's. Yes, I heard the news. I did not mean to suggest that I didn't know. Blessings to you and your family."

"Why do you want to talk with Kejal?"

"I need his help."

"To do what?" the woman asked.

"I can't really say."

"Then I can't really tell you how to reach him."

"No, no, please don't hang up. I really need to speak to him. It's a matter of life and death."

"You want to kill Kejal, don't you? What did he do this time? Not chop off the heads of the people you commanded him to? I'm sure if he is hiding, then it is for good reason. And I'm not exactly inclined to give you his number. You probably have it already, but he isn't answering your calls."

"No, no. That's not it at all. I'm not with Al Hasib."

"Of course you'd say you weren't. I'm not falling for that."

"Is Kejal there?"

"If he was, I wouldn't tell you. Now, leave me alone, and don't ever call here again."

Hawk hung up, disappointed over the rejection from the woman that he figured was Kejal's mother and Jaziri's sister. Al Hasib had torn her family apart, and she suspected Hawk was affiliated with the terrorists. While lamenting the inability to connect with Kejal through his family, Hawk understood the woman's reticence to help.

Hawk was convinced that pressing her would only make it worse, especially if Al Hasib was listening in on her conversations or if Kejal really had abandoned his post with the group. Instead of wasting more time in what Hawk suspected would be a futile effort, he reported the news back to Fortner.

"We don't have much time now," Fortner said. "We need to come up with another plan."

"I'm already on it," Hawk said.

CHAPTER 10

NOAH YOUNG TOOK A FEW practice swings with his golf club while waiting just off the cart path for his playing partner. A grin spread across his face as he saw Brady Hawk approaching on another cart driven by a member of Young's secret service detail. Once the vehicle came to a stop, Hawk climbed out and strode toward the president.

"How did you rig this?" Hawk asked as he put on his gloves.

"I just told them that I was going to play with a guy who could drive the ball with such force that he could easily kill a person, though he never could tell where the ball would go," Young said with a chuckle.

"That's actually pretty accurate," Hawk said. "Fortunately, this is a ruse, is it not? Because you'd take all the money in my pocket and the shirt off my back if we were betting on a round of golf."

"It's all right," Young said. "We'll probably only

need the time it takes to play three holes to discuss this. And you're up first."

Hawk shook his head. "You're really gonna make me play, aren't you?"

"Purely for entertainment purposes only. It would bring me great personal satisfaction to know that there's at least one physical activity I can do better than Brady Hawk."

Hawk chuckled as he shoved his tee into the ground and balanced a ball on top. After a few swings to loosen up, he prepared to take his first shot.

"This hole plays long," Young said. "Don't think about trying to lay up around that pond there."

Hawk shot Young a sideways glance before recoiling and unleashing a blistering shot. The ball whistled over the pond on the par four hole, landing less than fifty yards from the green.

Hawk winked at Young as they passed near the base of the tee box.

"You're a golf shark," Young said. "And to think I was very close to falling for it."

Hawk shrugged. "I got decent at golf on Uncle Sam's dime while waiting for training school to get started. They called it casual status. Make a few pots of coffee in the morning and play loads of golf in the afternoon."

Young grunted as he set up his ball. He barely

got the ball over the pond, but he remained in good shape for his next shot.

"It's not how you start but how you finish," Young said.

They both climbed into the same cart with driving privileges taken by Young.

"I guess it's time to get down to the real meaning for this golf outing," Hawk said.

Young adjusted his sunglasses and tugged at the sleeves on his jacket. "I appreciate you coming out because I've got a real problem, Hawk. *We* have a real problem."

"And what's that?"

"Someone recorded Daniels's dying moments, and there's a guy who's essentially blackmailing me over it."

"Blackmailing you? That takes some guts. Do you know who he is?"

"Not sure yet, but his identity isn't what has me worried—it's what he plans to do with the footage if I don't tell the American people what really happened with Daniels."

"There's a reason we never told anyone in the first place."

"I know," Young said as he averted a jarring pothole. "I tried to tell him that. We didn't want Daniels to lose his dignity in death. Once that video goes public, it'll forever be in the public sphere, available on the Internet for all of time. We obviously didn't see eye to eye on a lot of issues, but I still wouldn't want Daniels disparaged like that."

"What were this mystery man's demands?"

"I need to tell the truth or he's going to take the footage public."

"Do you believe him?"

Young threw his head back, scratching underneath his chin. "He seemed pretty intent on following through."

"And he didn't ask for money?"

"No, which was strange. So, I guess it's not technically a blackmail when we're looking at it from a legal perspective."

"He's still coercing you to do something against your will. And that's technically blackmail."

Young furrowed his brow as he turned toward Hawk. "Were you also a lawyer and I'm just now finding out about this?"

Hawk stared off in the distance. "No, but I know all about blackmail. Just don't ask me how, okay?"

"If you insist."

Hawk put a tee in his mouth and gnawed on the sharp end for a moment before continuing the conversation.

"Let me ask you," Hawk began, "what are you

afraid will happen if this man releases the footage?"

"I've seen it, and it doesn't look good."

"Yeah, but *what* are you afraid of personally? Losing the election?"

Young thought for a moment. The question made him uncomfortable. Perhaps he was being selfish and using Daniels's dignity as a shield.

"I know what you're getting at," Young said. "The reason not to tell should be for the protection of others, not myself."

"Exactly. If the public perceives that you refused to tell the truth because you cared more about winning your office, it'll come back to haunt you. Besides, what are the latest polls showing? Aren't you up by a considerable amount?"

Young nodded. "It's hard to lose to a man whose son is a known traitor and attempted to assist a terrorist organization in attacking us on our own soil. I daresay that everyone in my campaign office thinks this election will be a cakewalk."

"At this point, the result seems like a foregone conclusion."

"And that's what I'm afraid of, if I'm being honest. That this easy victory will vanish and I'll be scrapping for my life the moment this news goes public."

"Better to get out in front of it than let it run you over."

Young eased onto the brakes. They squeaked as the cart halted just shy of his ball. With silent precision, he pulled out his eight iron and ripped a shot that landed less than a foot from the hole.

"Nice shot," Hawk said. "You've got some nerves of steel. I bet you can spin this story in a way that turns out to your advantage."

Young released the brake and sped toward Hawk's ball.

"You're probably right. I need to get over my fear and do it before I end up paying a steeper price for the backlash."

Hawk jumped out of the cart and watched his shot skip onto the green and roll to a stop five feet from the pin. He threw his club in the bag and climbed back inside the vehicle.

"But just in case things don't go the way I want them to go, I was wondering if you could do me a favor," Young said as he stepped on the gas pedal.

"What's that?"

"Find out who this guy is. Find out what his real motive is. Maybe he's an operative working for James Peterson. Maybe he's a family member with an axe to grind or some member of the press looking for a big exclusive."

"At this point, you can't worry about his motivation. You just need to do the right thing."

Young nodded and sighed. "But just in case—"

"Okay, I'll see what I can find out, but I want to go on the record as saying that I don't like this idea."

"Don't worry. I'll protect you from any blowback."

Hawk pulled his putter out of his bag. "The fact that you're even making that statement concerns me the most."

"It probably won't matter—it's just a backup plan."

"Let's hope you're right."

CHAPTER 11

Zagros Mountains, Iraq

KARIF FAZIL SIFTED THROUGH a stack of documents on his desk, looking for one in particular. After several minutes of searching, the title of the report caught his eye. He stopped and snatched the page out of the pile, reading every word intently. Fazil smiled as he picked up his phone and dialed Brady Hawk's number.

"Are you ready for further instructions?" Fazil said after Hawk answered.

"I'm not going to kill him for you. Let's just be clear about that up front."

"And I have already assured you that I will not ask you to do that."

"Is your word really that trustworthy?"

Fazil laughed softly. "Your two friends are still alive, are they not?"

"I don't know. I haven't seen or heard from them in a while."

"Just a moment."

Fazil typed a few things into his phone and pushed send.

"Check your phone," he said. "If you click on the link I sent you, you'll be able to see them and speak with them."

A few seconds later, Fazil watched a monitor showing his two prisoners. They waved at the camera capturing their every move and tried to speak.

"They can hear you, but you cannot hear them," Fazil said. "But I can assure you that they are eager to speak with you."

"I bet they are."

"So, does that satisfy your proof of life question?" Fazil asked.

"It'll do."

"In that case, we need to get down to business. You have much to do in the next couple days leading up to the assassination attempt on Noah Young's life."

"Getting close enough to the man currently serving as President of the U.S. won't be easy, if that's what you're thinking."

"You must not get ahead of yourself," Fazil said. "Take a deep breath, relax, and listen. I have all the plans taken care of, and your role is a simple but vital one. I need you to help one of my men gain access to Andrews Air Force Base without raising any suspicion."

The sound of Hawk chuckling came in clearly. "That's your big plan? What is your man going to do when he gets there? Getting arrested is imminent."

"My men will never be taken alive. I would think you would know that by now."

"Perhaps you're forgetting that we took one of your men recently while foiling another plan of yours in Colombia," Hawk said. "He's very much alive and eager to talk. From what I've heard, he'll do anything to get out of solitary confinement."

Fazil stroked his beard and pondered if he should reveal the truth about the prisoner. He decided against it and continued his banter with Hawk.

"Despite my best efforts, I cannot control everyone. If someone wants to leave Al Hasib for another group of jihadists, I will not try to stop them. There are also others who simply want to betray you. While I would have no mercy on such a man if he were to return, I understand that such men exist in the ranks of every military power on earth."

"You'd be hard pressed to find men who would betray their own country here," Hawk said.

"Is that a fact?" Fazil asked.

"Absolutely. The only thing more absurd than thinking there are a plethora of men—let alone a single man—who are just eager to betray their nation is the fact that you think I can help your man get close enough to the president."

Fazil hammered away on his cell's keyboard. "Check your phone for the picture I just sent you."

A few seconds later, Fazil heard an audible gasp come from the receiver.

"How did you—"

"That's not important," Fazil said. "My point is that you're wrong on both accounts. There are people eager to betray their own country, living in your midst and perhaps serving at the pleasure of the president himself. And you are far more than capable of getting close to the president, as evidenced by the photograph."

"Even if you are right, how is this going to help you assassinate President Young?"

"I can assure you that it will be spectacular. Television crews will be filming the president's flight to his final campaign rally in Texas when his plane will disintegrate right before everyone's eyes."

"You sick bastard," Hawk said. "You want your own 9-1-1 moment."

"And I'm going to have it with your help, that is if you want your two friends here to live."

"You can't possibly think you're going to get away with this, much less that I'll go along with you."

Fazil chuckled. "You have no choice now. Besides, Mr. Hawk, you have so much to learn about me and Al Hasib. No one ever embarks on a mission with the belief that they will return. Instead, they go with the hope of entering eternity as a martyred hero."

"I don't care what you believe," Hawk said. "What I'm saying is that you'll likely never even get an opportunity to take a shot. The President of the United States is one of the most heavily guarded men on the planet. Your presumption about an operation like this is astounding."

"That is why I have you on my side now, Mr. Hawk," Fazil said. "You're going to make sure that my man not only gains access to the grounds but also that no one sees him before he destroys Air Force One. If he fails to take the shot, I will take two shots at your friends, but only after they have been thoroughly tortured."

"After this is all over, I swear I'm going to—"

"What have I told you about making empty threats? It will do nothing but bring you further embarrassment. I'll be in touch."

Fazil hung up and grinned. Listening to Hawk get worked up brought on an inordinate amount of pleasure. But that's how Fazil liked it—rubbing his power and control in the faces of his enemies. He felt confident he would be doing the same thing to the entire world soon enough after he finished avenging the death of his brother.

He looked at Jafar and held his hand out. "Those two Americans are having a virtual vacation here. Let us go show them how we like to handle people who try to stand in our way."

With Jafar perched on Fazil's shoulder, the Al Hasib head lumbered down the hallway, excited about the prospect of roughing up Hawk's two favorite people in the world.

They will survive, but they will wish they were dead before I'm through with them.

CHAPTER 12

Zagros Mountains, Iraq

ALEX WAITED UNTIL THE DOOR rattled shut behind Fazil before she spit blood onto the cell floor. She looked at Blunt, whose left eye had already swelled up. He groaned as he shifted positions. While Fazil said little other than disparaging comments during the torture session, Alex wondered if beyond the prison walls the situation wasn't going as he planned.

The overhead pipes in the ten-foot by ten-foot cell dripped several times per minutes, enough to keep the air damp and a small puddle in the center of the room. Alex and Blunt stood with their arms chained to the wall. Their movement was limited, though Alex tried to jog in place to keep her blood moving.

She waited to speak until she was certain no guards were close enough to hear.

"You still hanging in there?" Alex asked.

Blunt grunted. "I'm too old for this."

"That's not what I asked," she said. "I need to know that you're still with me."

"What the hell for? It's not like we're going somewhere any time soon."

Alex took a deep breath and winced from the pain in her ribs. "We need to be if we're going to survive. Do you honestly think Fazil is going to let us live?"

Blunt shook his head. "We're as good as dead."

"And that's all the more reason for us to attempt an escape."

"We're chained to the wall, not to mention we have no idea where we are. Afghanistan, Iraq, Oman. Who the hell knows? If we get out, we'd probably be dead within the hour—or worse."

"Worse than dead?"

"Sometimes death is a merciful mistress."

Alex scowled. "I hope this doesn't mean that you're ready to throw in the towel because I'm certainly not."

"If we're dead, it means they can't hurt us any more. And I think so far, Fazil has been surprisingly kind to you. It's only a matter of time before things get far more unsavory for you, if you know what I mean."

"All the more reason for us to get out of here."

"Alex, they're just going to drag us back in here

and do more vile things to us—all before they kill us."

"From what you're saying, it sounds like we're damned if we do and damned if we don't. Quite frankly, I'd rather die trying than simply await some fate Fazil has dictated for us."

"So, you have a plan?"

"I guess you could say that," she said with a faint smile. "I've got an emergency tracking device in my shoe one of my friends at the CIA gave me."

"That could be a game changer. Why didn't you tell me about this earlier?"

"I wanted to wait and see what happened first before I used it, not to mention the battery life is very short. A couple hours at the most. So I wanted to make sure we weren't going to be moved around. And there hasn't been any indication that they have plans to take us somewhere else. Plus, I haven't really had a chance to talk about this since this is the first time there haven't been guards right outside the door."

Blunt nodded subtly. "Makes sense. Now, where exactly is this handy little gadget?"

"It's in the sole of my shoe."

"Can you activate it now?"

Alex laughed softly. "I'm fairly flexible, but I'm not a contortionist."

"So, how do you plan on turning that sucker on?"

"Tomorrow when they feed us, they unshackle

us. I'll try to do it then."

Blunt's eyes widened. "They usually have a guard or two in the room watching us."

"Maybe you'll have to get creative to distract him. I'm sure you're more than capable."

"I'll think of something."

Alex had more she wanted to say, but she decided against it when she heard the scuffing of footsteps headed toward them from down the hall.

She took a deep breath and readjusted her position once more, and a searing pain overtook her body. The combination of the beating and being forced to keep her hands raised above her head while standing was taking a toll on her, both physically and mentally.

You can do this, Alex. Just breathe.

CHAPTER 13

Washington, D.C.

HAWK STOOD IN THE WINGS of the stage that stretched across the south end of the Capital One Arena. Noah Young was still fifteen minutes away from kicking off his final rally in the nation's capital before the election, but the arena was packed and buzzing with excitement. News of a big forthcoming announcement from Young had the media whipped into a frenzy and the curious public wondering if this was just another overhyped political stunt.

Rolling up the program Hawk had picked up when he was in the hospitality suite, he tapped the paper against his leg. He looked at his watch again, the seconds dripping past slowly. Despite the importance of Young's announcement, Hawk was ready to move on and return his focus to the more pressing issue of how he was going to handle Karif Fazil's demands without killing the president.

Hawk studied Young, who stood in the corner and flipped through his speech notes. With relaxed shoulders and an expressionless demeanor, Young looked to be engaged in nothing more than a routine procedure like washing his hands or drinking a glass of water. Hawk searched for the slightest glint of sweat on Young's forehead yet noticed nothing. He looked up briefly when a senator came by and patted him on the back, saying something that elicited Young's megawatt smile.

Checking the time again, Hawk turned his focus toward one of Young's campaign aides, Emma Fulton. She was a rising star in Washington's political scene, mostly for her ability to help candidates connect with a new generation of voters. Hawk walked over to Emma, who was texting off and on, reacting quickly to each new message that popped up on her phone.

"You can't ever leave your work at work any more, can you?" Hawk asked.

She paused to cast a sideways glance at him. "Can't afford to. Someone else will take your job."

Hawk's attempt at small talk was just to break the ice so he could ask the question that he really wanted answered. His primary intention was to gauge her reaction about the forthcoming announcement by her candidate.

"So, what did you think when you heard the news?" he asked.

She didn't look up from her texting. "I'm afraid you're gonna have to be more specific than that with me."

"Sorry, I'm sure it probably doesn't even feel like news to you when you're on the inside. I was referring to Young's big announcement that he plans on making at this rally."

She shrugged. "I wish he would've said something earlier than waiting this late in the campaign."

"Do you think it's going to hurt him?"

"What? Waiting this late to announce it?" she asked before shaking her head. "It shouldn't matter with the voting public."

"But this will dominate the headlines for days. You don't think it will sway some folks?"

Emma looked warily at Hawk. "I don't know if you've seen the polls lately, but this election isn't going to be decided by last-minute undecided voters. This announcement will only give Young more credibility."

Hawk furrowed his brow. Emma had become known for her ability to spin a story, but he struggled to believe she could sugarcoat the truth surrounding Conrad Daniels's death.

"Now, if you'll excuse me, I've got another fire to put out," she said before walking away while hammering out another text.

Hawk killed the remaining time by staying in the shadows and watching the crowd anxious to begin the rally.

When Noah Young glided onto the stage to thunderous applause, he wore a big smile and waved in all directions. He sauntered over to the glass podium and waited for the cheering to die down before speaking.

"Thank you for that warm welcome," Young began, only to be interrupted by yet another twenty seconds of clapping.

Young raised his hands again, gesturing for the crowd to calm down. He then broke into his stump speech, reiterating the promises and points of focus that his campaign had drummed into the heads of voters who bothered to listen. Half an hour into the speech, Young had excited them. Hawk noted how the hope seemed almost palpable. Everyone in the building was going to leave with the idea that the future was bright if Young retained his position as president.

Then Young's tone turned somber. "In moving forward, we must not forget the man who came before me, President Conrad Daniels, God rest his soul."

Here we go. Hawk took a deep breath and closely watched the audience's reaction as Young continued.

"Before President Daniels's tragic death, there were a few pieces of legislation that he was passionate about. And one of those had to do with keeping the

American people safe from terrorists.

"Now, I know he wasn't perfect. He had his faults like anyone does. But I never once questioned his commitment to this country. And I can't think of a better way to honor his memory than opening up my presidency by passing a bill in his honor that will help us fight terrorism more effectively and keep this nation one of the safest on earth.

"The Daniels Act will grant further liberties for our troops and special forces attempting to ferret out and eliminate terrorist organizations, much like the one that recently made a failed attack on New York City. With the Daniels Act, our counterterrorism forces would've been able to act more swiftly and decisively in squelching the activities of these nefarious agents who try to do harm to this country. They would've never been able to even mount something akin to what we consider a credible threat.

"As someone who loves this country deeply, I want to ensure that the freedoms we've had for a couple of centuries remain in place for generations to come. Terrorists thrive on fear, but I want them to fear us. No longer will we cower at their efforts to bring chaos to our culture. No longer will we wonder when we'll experience the next attack. No longer will we be afraid."

Hawk watched the crowd rise to its feet and explode with applause. Young smiled and waved, raising both hands. He pumped his fists and spouted off a few campaign slogans, whipping the crowd to a fever pitch.

And then he walked off the stage.

That's not exactly how this was supposed to go.

Campaign aides and other staffers swarmed Young once he reached the stage wings. Hearty hugs and wide smiles marked the scene. If the speech had been a sporting event, Young would've certainly been carried off on the shoulders of his teammates while they chanted of his glory.

The corners of Hawk's mouth remained down, unwilling to even flash a grin despite the joyful celebration occurring a few feet away. Instead of being honest with the American people about what happened to Daniels, Young chose to bask in the adulation. Hawk couldn't really blame Young either. The crowd could feel the energy, the surging momentum that swept them all away. Though the label sounded cliché to Hawk, *hope* was the best way to describe how everyone in the building felt.

But all Hawk could see was the closet in the background, looming over Young and waiting to be opened. Everything was on the verge of being swept away. If Young's blackmailer decided to make the video public, the campaign moment everyone had just experienced would be a footnote, if not all forgotten. And Hawk sensed he needed to remind Young of that fact.

"That was a moving speech," Hawk said, shaking Young's hand.

"It was almost as if I was feeding off of them," Young said.

"You were feeding them something because they were eating out of your hand."

Young flashed a grin. "Selling hope has a way of doing that with people, though I believe every word of what I just said."

"Well, it's not what you said that got my attention. It's what you didn't say."

Young grabbed Hawk by the arm and led him farther away from the cluster of aides that had formed nearby.

"Look, about that—"

"You better pray that man hasn't pushed the button yet and published that video to social media," Hawk warned. "If he did, this entire event won't get a single minute of air time. It'll all be an endless cycle of that footage of you and Daniels, and you know it."

"I can't do it—at least, not before the election. It's only a few days away."

Hawk eyed Young closely. "But didn't you tell me that the man gave you a deadline that was before the election? I don't think you want this story gaining traction a few days before the vote."

Young clenched his teeth. "I'm the President of the United States, and I'll be damned if I'm going to let someone bully me."

"I want to go on record as saying I think it's a bad idea to ignore this guy."

"I'm not ignoring him. In fact, I'm giving him more attention than he ever dreamed of getting."

"And how are you doing that?"

"I'm sending you to pay him a little visit and take care of the problem."

"But, sir, I—"

Young slapped Hawk on the arm. "Thanks, Hawk. I knew I could count on you."

Hawk sighed. "Well, there's something else I need to talk with you about."

An aide rushed up to Young and whispered something in his ear. "It's gonna have to wait. Duty calls. But give Big Earv a call. I had him start digging into the guy."

Hawk watched Young stride off as he spoke with several advisors. In that moment, Young appeared presidential to Hawk. No longer was Young the man behind the scenes pulling all the strings. He'd ascended to the steps of the throne and was angling to have a seat for four—perhaps even eight—years.

But Hawk knew every aspiration Young had of moving into the Oval Office would permanently be dashed if he didn't deal directly with the man who was blackmailing him. Hawk didn't want to be the one to handle it either, given the other extenuating circumstances that were far more pressing.

He turned to leave but noticed Young had stopped to take a picture with a woman backstage. At first glance, Hawk didn't recognize her. But then as he took a second look, he realized who she was—Deepika Padukone. Hawk doubted hardly anyone would recognize the Bollywood star out on the street, but he did. And he wasn't about to let his opportunity to take a picture with her go to waste.

For a moment, he felt sheepish about fawning over a famous actress. But Hawk got over it, telling himself that he was doing it for Alex.

She'll think this is great.

He asked Padukone if she minded posing for a picture, which she readily agreed to. Moments later, Hawk was headed for the exits while he stared at the photo of Padukone on his phone. He couldn't wait to show Alex. Then he had another thought.

I hope Alex is still alive for me to show her this picture.

He turned off his phone and slid it into his pocket. Hawk had plenty of things to do before he could start pondering if Fazil would keep his word.

CHAPTER 14

Zagros Mountains, Iraq

KARIF FAZIL SHOOK HIS HEAD as he watched the report about Noah Young's speech on terrorism that the newscaster described as "stirring and inspiring." Fazil considered the rhetoric nothing more than empty talk, the kind of message that would only excite his current base of supporters. Though Young sounded benign politically, Fazil didn't miss Young's opening salvo. If elected, Young had promised to make terrorists' lives difficult through an aggressive campaign.

Too bad you won't be able to follow through on your promise.

Fazil studied several documents detailing the next steps in his plan once the U.S. election was thrown into disarray. Once there was a vacuum of leadership, Fazil recognized there would be an optimum window of opportunity to strike. And Al Hasib needed to strike fast and furiously. He understood enough about the American political culture to know that the nation's attention would be zeroed in on avoiding a constitutional crisis, just like the one the country almost had with Daniels's death. Only this would be much worse. All Fazil needed to do now was wait for the first domino to fall. Once Young was dead, chaos would ensue.

"Come, come, Jafar," Fazil said, snapping his fingers to signal for the bird to join him. "We must check in with Youssef and make sure he has everything he needs to—how do they say it in America?—get the party started?"

Fazil punched in Youssef Nawabi's phone number and pressed send, waiting patiently for the marksman to answer.

"Alo," Nawabi answered.

"How are your preparations coming along?" Fazil asked, being discreet as possible in what he said.

"There have not been any surprises yet, so I guess you could say that they are going well."

"You must stay vigilant," Fazil said. "Nothing ever runs smoothly—at least, nothing ever runs as smoothly as you'd like."

"I expect disruptions any day now and am ready for whatever might be thrown my way."

"Excellent. You must be on guard. Our entire mission is counting on you. Once you remove their leader, we can begin to move into phase two of our plan."

"How is your training coming along? Have you been able to practice as you had hoped?"

"I believe I'm ready. The past few days I have fine tuned my skills, though I'm not sure anything can prepare me fully for the moment."

"I know you will be ready. Keep me informed on any changes. I'll send you the details for the next meeting with your liaison there."

Fazil was proud of Nawabi and the journey he began after his brother was killed at the hands of Brady Hawk. Nawabi approached Fazil about training for one of Al Hasib's special missions. At first, Fazil wasn't sure if Nawabi simply wanted revenge—something Fazil would certainly never hold against anyone—or if he genuinely wanted to help the cause. After a few months of watching Nawabi grow from a fighter in the trenches to one of the best shots with an RPG in the ranks of Al Hasib, the answer was clear.

Fazil always had several missions running, some active while others were of the long-range variety. Sleeper cells, deep cover, infiltrating the U.S. military ranks—they were the kind of operations he needed to prepare for in case he had the opportunity to strike swiftly. Nawabi had been preparing to put his training into action for more than six months, and Fazil had little doubt that his most skilled shooter was prepared. On top of Nawabi's excellent ability to hit targets with his RPG, he was also a solid marksman. He regularly hit his target from 800 yards, which was enough to help Al Hasib advance as it attempted to besiege several strongholds in Iraq and Afghanistan. Nawabi had thrown a few mundane afternoons in several villages into complete chaos based on his long-range shooting ability. Fazil always preferred the silent assassin, though such a tactic wasn't always the best. Nawabi's ability helped Fazil cover both options with one soldier.

Fazil said a quick prayer underneath his breath for Nawabi. The last thing Fazil wanted was to lose his prized asset before Nawabi ever got off a shot. But Fazil knew Nawabi was as good as gone the moment he left for the U.S. If Nawabi did his job, he'd die a martyr's death, joining his brother in eternity. It was what Fazil wanted, but he couldn't deny a soldier unafraid to stare death in the face for Al Hasib's *jihad* cause.

Fazil paused for a moment before hanging up, adding one final instruction.

"When you meet your contact, control yourself," Fazil said. "I know you're going to want to kill him, but please refrain. Your mission will be in vain if you attempt anything, plus you will have to deal with my wrath should you return."

"Your wrath? Don't you want him out of the picture?" Nawabi asked.

"I want him eliminated almost more than anything—but I want to be the one to do it. If you bring him back with you, make sure he is still kicking. If not, there will be serious repercussions for your actions. Is that clear?"

"I understand," Nawabi said.

"I didn't ask if you understand. I want to know if you think my instructions are clear—and that you plan to abide by them?"

Fazil waited out an awkward moment of silence before Nawabi finally spoke.

"They are clear, sir, and I will abide by them."

"Good, that is what I was hoping to hear," Fazil said before he hung up the phone.

I have my own special plans for Brady Hawk.

CHAPTER 15

Zagros Mountains, Iraq

ALEX WAS CERTAIN BLUNT could hear her stomach growling. Hours had passed since they last receive rations of any kind, much less a drink of water. So torturous was the lack of liquids that Alex eyed the puddle in the cell floor and licked her lips.

If only I could get close enough to that water . . .

The shuffling of feet in the distance snapped Alex out of her delusional state. She hoped that the guard heading toward them had something for them to eat and drink.

"You ready?" whispered Blunt.

"Ready as I'll ever be," she said.

"Just be careful, okay? If you don't have a good opportunity now, you can try again later. That device is our lone silver bullet at this point."

"One we need to fire right away if we're gonna

have a chance."

"Just be patient."

Alex sighed and chewed on her lip. She was glad she wasn't alone. Having Blunt in the cell helped her not lose her mind—and her patience. She knew he was right, but she didn't like waiting, especially in a situation like this. Escaping her shackles was her top priority because eventually Fazil would turn his men loose on her. And that wasn't something she wanted to experience.

The guard jangled his keys, taking his time to find the right one before inserting it into the lock. With a loud echo, the deadbolt clicked open and the hinges creaked as the guard pushed his way into the room.

"Have food for you," he said in his broken English. "Hungry?"

Alex nodded and then glanced at her shackles.

"Oh, I help you."

He set down the tray of food in the center of the room, directly in the path of the dripping pipe. Alex watched as water splattered on the food. In most cases, her stomach would've turned at such a sight, but she shrugged it off, too hungry to care.

The guard fiddled with her chains for a few moments until he finally unlocked them, allowing her to move freely again. Her eyes met his, and he tapped the gun holstered in his belt. He then wagged his finger, his insinuation clear. She nodded and shook her hands for a few moments before kneeling down next to the tray and collecting a plate.

She eyed the guard as he proceeded to work on Blunt's chains. For a second, she contemplated ripping her shoe off and activating the homing beacon while the guard wasn't looking. But her gaze met Blunt's, and he nodded subtly.

Be patient, he says.

Alex wanted to growl and hit something. But she knew Blunt's approach was the one that gave her a better chance at success. One misstep and the man would have her tracking device. And nothing good would come of that.

After the guard freed Blunt, he gestured down toward the food.

"You take and eat," the guard said.

Blunt nodded and stooped down to collect his plate just before another drop soiled his food even further.

"Thank you," Alex said as she stuffed her face. "I was hungry."

"Is good?" the guard asked.

"Yes," she said with her mouth half full.

Less than a minute later, she was finished. What exactly she had eaten, she wasn't sure, nor was she interested in finding out. A paisley-colored soup that was thin and bland along with a stone-hard biscuit and a cup of water. But it didn't matter to Alex. She was simply content to put anything in her stomach.

While Blunt scarfed down his food, the next order of business for Alex was going to the bathroom. The lack of liquids didn't put her in emergency situation, but she had been holding her pee for longer than she wanted.

The single toilet against the wall was moldy and didn't appear to have been cleaned in months, if not years. The pungent odor of stale piss permeated the room when she put the lid down to use the restroom.

Forcing a smile, she looked at the guard and turned to take a seat. But the guard didn't move.

"Do you mind?" Alex said. "I have to pee."

She gestured with her hand for him to turn around.

"I sorry. I must watch whole time. Orders from boss."

She sighed. "Really?"

He nodded, almost apologetically.

"Fine," she said, ripping her pants down and sitting on the toilet seat as quickly as possible, careful not to expose herself so openly.

She glanced over at Blunt, who had turned his back to her in an apparent effort to give her some privacy. Meanwhile, the guard focused all his attention on Alex. Due to the language barrier, he came across as dopey to her, but she could tell he was more creep than dolt. His gaze didn't move off her for the entire time she was sitting down.

So much for that plan.

For a second, she contemplated leaping off the toilet and shoving the guard backward over Blunt so that the soldier would topple to the ground. But once she considered it fully, she wasn't sure she'd have the time necessary to remove the tracker and activate it before guards descended upon the cell. And if she failed, there wasn't going to be a second chance.

"Do you mind?" Alex said as she prepared to stand up.

The guard didn't flinch. "No. Please."

She rolled her eyes and shimmied her pants up as quickly as possible to prevent the pervert from seeing anything. He smiled at her.

"Thank you," he said.

"I swear you better hope we don't meet outside of this prison."

"Thank you," he said again.

She let out an exasperated breath and took one last swig of the water remaining in her cup.

"Remember what I said, Alex," Blunt said. "Be patient."

"I know, I know. But I really just want to go

ballistic up against the side of this guy's head."

"So do I, but we can't—at least, not right now. Just stay the course."

The guard glanced at the chains and then back at Alex. She knew what to do. She set the clamp over her wrists and held them up for the guard so he could lock them down. Once the bindings clicked into place, she watched him reattach the chains on Blunt.

I guess this idea is officially tabled for now.

"You need anything?" the guard asked as he moved to the doorway.

"A bigger portion of food and then a map on how to get out of this place."

The guard smiled. "Tomorrow?"

"Okay," Alex said, surprised that he even responded, though she was certain he was just going through the routine of asking questions he was trained to ask.

Then the guard did something that surprised her even more: he spoke in perfect English.

"I'm not sure what you are planning, but I suggest you reconsider. Fighting against anything Karif Fazil wants to do is pointless and will only mean a more painful death for you in the end." He pointed to the camera in the corner of the room. "We will be watching you."

Alex glared at him. Any warm feelings she'd had toward him vanished the instant he stopped talking. He was creepy *and* sneaky, which was a repulsive combination to her. His act had fooled Alex and embarrassed her.

The guard placed Blunt back in his chains before collecting the tray and the empty dishes. He whistled as he moved everything outside and locked the door.

"Sweet dreams," he said before walking down the hall.

After the door shut behind the guard at the end of the hallway, Blunt spoke.

"If it makes you feel any better, Alex, I didn't see that coming either. We both got duped, I'm afraid."

"At least we didn't directly reference the *thing*."

"Of course not. I wouldn't do that, and I hope you wouldn't either. For all we know, they're watching *and* listening to us right now."

"He made a specific point to say they would be watching us," Alex said. "He was very particular about all his word choices, so it makes me think that they can only see us."

"If that's the case, you'll have to be discreet," Blunt said. "But I'm still wondering how you're going to execute everything."

"I'll figure something out."

Alex spent the next half hour studying the room and thinking up a way to get her shoe off her foot, inch it up to her hands, and remove the device and activate it—all without drawing the attention of any guard who was watching her on the security feed. After much thought, Alex developed a plan.

Without saying a word to Blunt, she removed both her shoes, clawing at her heels with her toes to free her shoes up. She let them lie haphazardly in front of her and moved her feet around, flexing her toes and doing a little half-hearted dance. After that she waited and waited.

Another half hour passed before she made another move.

This time, Alex used her toes to snatch the heel of the right shoe and pulled it back against the wall. She pinned the shoe against the wall with her butt and slowly worked the shoe upward, all while maintaining a motion that would appear to anyone watching that she was itching her back. After fifteen painful minutes, she maneuvered the shoe up near her head. This enabled her to grab the shoe. She worked to dig out the cushion but with little luck. The cushion remained stuck inside the shoe.

As she worked on this, the main door to the prison opened, echoing down the hallway.

She cursed under her breath and mulled over her decision: continue to dig out the device and hope a guard doesn't enter the prison or drop the shoe immediately and hope it doesn't fall too far away. Alex opted for the former.

Come on. Get outta there.

She scraped at the edges frantically while the footfalls grew closer and closer.

Just a little more.

As the cushion broke free, the sound of a key being inserted into her cell's lock sent her into a panic. Her hands started to sweat and the shoe slipped free, the device still inside.

A guard strode into the room and glared at Alex.

"Do you need to go to the restroom?" he asked in perfect English. "You looked like you might be in pain."

Alex grimaced and played along. "Oh, yes, thank you. I've had to go for quite a while now."

He unlocked her chains and remained in the cell.

"Do you mind?" she said.

He turned around to give her privacy and noticed one of her shoes lying in the middle of the room. Grunting as he stooped down to pick it up, he studied the inside.

"I think you dropped something," he said.

He stopped and inspected the shoe, digging at the misplaced sole.

"What's this?" he asked with a furrowed brow.

Alex shimmied her pants up and buttoned them quickly. She reached for the shoe.

"It's just a shoe. An uncomfortable one, but nothing more."

The guard pulled it back from her. "I don't think so. This looks like some sort of electronic device."

"It's just a battery-powered air freshener to keep my feet from grossing everyone out."

"No," he said. "I'm on to you. Up against the wall."

Alex sighed and complied, knowing she had no chance in a fight against the bulky guard.

"They're going to make fun of you," she said as she slid her hands into the bindings. "Bringing a woman's shoe back because you think there's some dangerous electronic device in it."

The guard chuckled. "Nobody makes fun of me. I can assure you of that."

Alex watched as he reattached her chains to the wall and exited the room, the door clanging shut behind him. She looked over at Blunt, who was shaking his head.

"Alex, Alex, Alex," he said with a groan.

"I know," she said. "It's all my fault. I thought I had it, but I was wrong."

"That's going to be a costly mistake, maybe even a deadly one."

She sighed. "You don't need to tell me that."

Her head dropped as she looked down at the floor, her other shoe still neatly in its place just below her. The water from the pipe splashed down into the small puddle as the full weight of her situation hit home.

We're both going to die.

CHAPTER 16

Washington, D.C.

HAWK TUCKED A COPY of *The Washington Post* under his arm and sauntered along one of the National Mall walkways. He scuffed at some of the pebbles marking the footpath as he moved toward his eventual location, a bench with its back to the Smithsonian Museum of Natural History and its front facing the Smithsonian Castle. Without any leaves on the trees, Hawk couldn't help but notice how bare the area was in December. Outside of the winter months, the trees were bursting with color and provided plenty of shade on those scorching afternoons for tourists visiting the nation's capital. But both the shade and tourists were in short supply as Hawk meandered along.

Before he sat down, Hawk attached an envelope beneath the bench next to his. He had stuffed the envelope in the newspaper, which he dropped to make his attempt at a quasi-dead drop seem more natural. Finished with his task, Hawk eased onto the bench and leaned back. He opened his paper and started to read about the latest on the election and the polls attempting to predict the outcome. Two minutes into an editorial opining about the potential makeup of Noah Young's cabinet, Hawk's appointment guest arrived.

Hawk peered over the top of his paper at the man and asked him a question to verify his identity.

"I don't know what's colder—this weather or the future?"

"Everything feels colder when you live under a repressive regime," the man answered.

Hawk sighed. He didn't make up the phrasing of the questions or the answers. They were the instructions Fazil had passed along. Hawk was sure the response was given just to irk him. Hawk tried to ignore it, but the phony exchange underscored why he wanted so badly to eliminate Al Hasib.

"Nice day for a walk," the man said.

"I'm not here for small talk, just business. You can practice your conversational English with someone else who gives a damn. I'm only here because I have to be."

"Very well then. Did you get the proper credentials?"

"They're located underneath your bench along

with a map of Andrews Air Force Base. What's your weapon?"

"I was instructed not to speak with you about such things."

Hawk huffed. "If you want to actually have a realistic shot at knocking Air Force One out of the sky, I need to know what weapon you have. Otherwise, I'm just throwing darts blindfolded."

"Fine," the man said after mulling the question over for a few seconds. "I plan on using an RPG-18e."

"Oh, state of the art," Hawk said. "You Al Hasib boys don't skimp on anything, do you?"

"Are you familiar with the weapon and its range?"

"I'm more than familiar with anything manufactured by Colton Industries. But that particular missile launcher is one I'm very acquainted with. I think I used it once to take out several Al Hasib strongholds on one mission I was on."

Hawk cut a sideways glance at the man to see if he would be distracted by the not-so-subtle jab. He wasn't.

"The guided missile system gives me an accuracy range of up to 2,000 meters, maybe even more."

"I figured you would be using a weapon with a distance somewhere in that vicinity. So, I took the liberty of marking a spot for you on the map for where you'll want to be in order to get the best unobstructed shot."

"And where is that?"

"There are several hangars near the end of the runway where Air Force One would lurch skyward. The target would be in plain view."

"What if I wanted to shoot him while the president was still on the ground?"

"You could probably do that, too, if you so desired. But I wouldn't recommend it. No guarantee of death. You miss by just a little bit, you'll never get another shot. With the plane, on the other hand, you only have to hit any part of that giant bird and you are going to get what you came for. There's no way anyone could survive a fall from that height."

"Thank you for your advice, but I like to keep my options open. You never know when things might change and you will need to come up with a different plan."

"From the sound of things, I think you've done this before."

The man didn't stop to bask in Hawk's faint praise. "I know I'll only get one shot. If I succeed, I will die. If I fail, I will die. I would prefer to be remembered as a success."

"In that case, you'll need to listen to my advice. Your credentials are inside the envelope, and you won't get near the base without them. In fact, you will look very suspicious trying to get on base without them. And if they sense something is off with you, they'll pull you out of your car and interrogate you. You'll be powerless to stop it. So keep your head up and act like you belong."

"Is that all I need to know?"

"I would recommend going to the base tomorrow and planting your weapon in one of the hangars. Carrying a weapon onto the base the day the president is flying out on Air Force One will also draw unwarranted attention."

"You make it sound so simple," the man said.

"Believe me when I say this, but it will be anything but simple. The kind of good fortune you're going to need just to get off a shot is rare, though possible. And then to actually hit the plane when the pressure is on—that will be up to you."

"I trust my weapon, especially the missile guided system that enables me to make such long shots from great distances. I once hit a squirrel's nest from fifteen hundred meters. I'm confident hitting Air Force One will not be a problem. I will get revenge, that I am sure of."

Hawk shook his head and sighed. "I would say *good luck*, but we both know I wouldn't mean it."

With his final salvo, Hawk stood and walked

away, refusing to look back at the man. His image was burned into Hawk's memory. And Hawk wasn't about to forget his face—until the Al Hasib assassin was dead.

CHAPTER 17

Washington, D.C.

NOAH YOUNG HAD A CHARMED political existence, which explained why he struggled with how
to handle the blackmailer. When Young first decided
to enter politics, he ran unopposed for the Texas state
representative position for Oldham County, a rural
county in the northwest part of the state. During his
second term, he struck up a friendship with George
Miller, who was a rising star in state politics. When
Miller became governor two years later, the two
worked closely together on various legislation initia-
tives. However, Young's big break didn't come until
Pip Haskins, the eighty-two-year-old U.S. senator from
Dallas, dropped dead of a heart attack near the end
of his sixth term.

Miller ignored his party's recommendations on
replacing Haskins with a retread politician with a

strong name brand among the base supporters. Instead, Miller said he wanted to shake things up and send some fresh ideas to Washington in the form of Noah Young. Young had a little less than a year before a special election was scheduled to determine if Miller's appointment would be more permanent or outright rejected by the people.

Young viewed his appointment to the U.S. Senate as the opportunity of a lifetime. In true Texas fashion, he seized the bull by the horns, making the most of his time in Washington. His charismatic oratory skills earned him a reputation as one of the most inspiring speakers among either party and often earned invitations to address various groups in non-partisan settings. In three months' time, Young's star was not just shooting but skyrocketing. And when Conrad Daniels sought out a running mate, Young's name landed at the top of the list.

If young were forced to admit it, the fact that he'd landed in Washington at all was a stroke of good fortune that he couldn't cajole into happening ever again, even if he wanted to.

Right place, right time.

Young marveled at the fact that he was on the precipice of winning a presidential election, the first one he would've won against someone from an opposing party for the first time in his career. He could almost taste it, though the blackmailer's demands made sure everything was bitter.

A knock at his basement office door jolted Young out of his trance.

"Come in," he said.

Brady Hawk strode into the room, shut the door, and took a seat across the desk from Young.

"I appreciate you helping me with this issue," Young began. "I'm not used to handling scrutiny like this."

"With all due respect, sir, this isn't exactly scrutiny," Hawk said. "You initiated a cover up and for good reason. I wholeheartedly supported the idea of fibbing to the American people on this one. We both know that the truth about Daniels's death really doesn't matter. He killed himself, plain and simple. That much is even evident on the footage. But somehow the cat has gotten out of the bag, and you cannot play around with this any more. Don't forget with Nixon that the cover up was greater than the actual crime."

"I appreciate your frankness, Hawk, but I still think the story we've foisted onto the American people is worth fighting for. Do we really want history to remember someone who once held the office of president as a weak-minded man who took the easy way out when confronted with his failings?"

Hawk shrugged. "What I find curious is your newly discovered affection for Daniels. You couldn't wait to push him out the door, also another decision I agreed with. He was harming our country with his reckless policies on how to combat extremists in the Middle East. Another four years of Daniels and this nation might have been on the brink of another world war. Given your change of heart, I can't help but wonder if you're afraid of how you'll be viewed since you're inextricably tied to him in the annals of history or if you're fearful that it might cost you the election. Care to shed some light on this change of heart you've had?"

Young clasped his hands and rested them on his desk. He paused pensively before responding. "Since you put it that way, my perception has changed on both accounts that you mentioned. If I admit that we covered up Daniels's death, people might start digging into the reality about what was going on with this administration's policies. And I know history wouldn't look favorably upon either of us if Daniels's true intentions were exposed. Then there's the matter of the election coming up in a few days. This would be a bombshell unlike any other we've ever seen in a presidential election in this country."

"You believe it would supplant the bombshell that your opponent's son helped a known terrorist into the country so he could detonate a nuclear weapon in the middle of New York?"

"Yes, I believe it would."

"At this point, what difference does it make? Peterson won't be able to score any political points on the issue of homeland security. So no matter what any journalist uncovered, it wouldn't hold the weight necessary to derail potential voters, much less penetrate the collective voters' consciousness to the point that people will flip to the other candidate. This election is a freight train and is chugging full speed down the tracks."

"If this guy is getting information on me like this, he must be well connected. And that frightens me more than anything. Who is really behind all this? It can't just be some random guy who's concerned about helping the truth get out there. No, I think it's something more."

Hawk suppressed a chuckle. "Don't let the conspiracy theorist in you run rampant around in your mind. And as far as we know, it's just a guy who managed to get your attention and wants the American people to know the truth. One good thing is that he's not a journalist or else this would be splashed over every news site from here to Seattle by now."

"I just want him taken care of, okay? Deal with it like you normally deal with problems."

"I hope you're not suggesting what I think you're suggesting."

Young templed his fingers, resting them against his lips. "Your methods are of no concern to me. I just want results, that's all. I want this man to go away." Young handed Hawk a folder. "We dug up a few more things on this guy, but I'm not sure how much it will help. We still don't know where he lives. He did a great job at evading the Secret Service tail I put on him."

Hawk opened up the folder and started reading. Nothing stood out to him as he glanced at the information, so he shut it abruptly.

"I'll handle this for you," Hawk said, "but we have more pressing issues to discuss."

"More pressing than this?" Young said, gesturing toward the folder. "This is my political future. Hell, the future of the nation hangs in the balance of this election. I can't imagine anything being more important than this."

"You're gonna need a bigger imagination then."

Young's eyes widened. "What's going on, Hawk?"

"I didn't want to mention this because I thought I could figure a way out of this, but it's apparent that I can't—at least, not without your help."

"What are you talking about?"

"Al Hasib kidnapped Blunt and Alex a few days ago."

"How did this happen?"

"It's a long story, sir, but the abbreviated version is that they used Colton to get at me, all for the sole purpose of forcing me to do something for them in exchange for the lives of Blunt and Alex."

"And you're going to do this thing for them?"

Hawk shook his head. "Not a chance."

"What do they want you to do?"

"Help someone assassinate you."

"What?"

"You heard me, sir. I didn't want to bother you with this because of everything you're focused on right now, but I can't wait any longer. There are some things already set into motion, and I need you to be prepared for what's going to happen."

"And what exactly is going to happen?"

"You're going to survive an assassination attempt."

"I don't like where this is going."

"Trust me, I don't either. But it might work out to your benefit. We might be able to kill two birds with one stone if we manage this situation properly."

"I hope you know what you're doing, Hawk. I'm not happy about a plan like this. But if anyone has earned the benefit of the doubt in a situation like this, you have."

"Don't worry, sir. I'm going to find a way out of

this mess and keep you alive in the process. I just thought you should know."

"Thanks for the heads up," Young said with a tinge of sarcasm.

Hawk ended the meeting by wishing Young good luck and promising to resolve the issue of the black-mailer.

Young watched the door to his office close as he spiraled back into thoughts about the blackmailer who was trying to derail Young's presidential aspirations. If only he wasn't *in* the video, which made him look more guilty. If he'd just waited until Daniels was dead, the evidence against Young wouldn't appear to be so damning.

Wrong place, wrong time.

CHAPTER 18

Springfield, Virginia

HAWK PARKED ALONG THE CURB in front of the one-story brick ranch and turned off his car along with the headlights. After grabbing the folder from the front passenger seat and switching on the dome light, he sifted through the Secret Service dossier prepared on Jared Fowler, the identity of Young's blackmailer.

At first glance, nothing set off alarm bells for Hawk regarding Fowler. The twenty-seven-year-old majored in business at Georgetown and graduated with honors five years ago. Since then, he started working at a real estate development firm and was responsible for several deals that resulted in the revitalization of a handful of Washington metro area neighborhoods. Fowler didn't have any parking tickets to his name, much less a criminal record.

The most curious thing was that Fowler had no

known connections to the White House or Secret Service. However, this concerned Hawk. Video footage like the kind Fowler had doesn't just tumble into someone's hands on accident—not unless he happened to be there. And since Fowler was a virtual Boy Scout, Hawk questioned just how in-depth the report was. Hawk was convinced something was missing.

"Where's the connection?" Hawk asked aloud. He pondered this question for a few more minutes but came up with nothing. He tucked the file away and climbed out of the car.

Hawk donned a fedora and put on a pair of fake glasses as he strode up the steps to Fowler's home and rapped hard on the screen door frame.

"I'm coming, I'm coming," a man said.

When the door swung open, Hawk didn't waste any time addressing the man.

"Jared Fowler?" Hawk asked.

"Yeah. Who are you?"

"I stopped by to speak with you on behalf of the president."

Fowler glanced down at his dinner plate and set it on a table in the entryway. He brushed the crumbs off his hands by clapping them together and ran his tongue around mouth before opening the door.

"I guess if you're here on behalf of the president, I ought to listen," Fowler said.

"Thanks," Hawk said as he ducked inside.

"Right this way," Fowler said, gesturing toward the adjacent sitting room. "And I'm sorry, I didn't catch your name."

"Max Summerton," Hawk said, giving an alias without skipping a beat. "I'm an advisor to the president, and he asked me to stop by and speak with you."

"I would ask how you found me, but that would be a stupid question."

Hawk sat down across from Fowler and chuckled. "There's not a lot the president can't find out about anyone, even those who come to him anonymously."

"Look, I don't want any trouble, and I'm not here to throw a fly in the political ointment just before the election. I just want the American people to know the truth out of respect for the office. And it's with that same respect that I wanted to give Vice-Pres—I mean, President Young—the opportunity to tell the truth about what happened to President Daniels."

"Help me understand why this is so important to you."

"Do you like to be lied to?"

Hawk shrugged. "I don't prefer it, but I realize it happens all the time. For instance, you could be lying to me right now."

"I could, but I'm also recording this encounter

in case something happens to me."

Hawk cocked his head to one side. "If you don't turn off your recording device, this meeting is over. I might say some things that aren't for the general public but for your benefit."

"Fine," Fowler said as he stood and grabbed the phone in the corner of the room. "It's off now. See?" He showed the phone to Hawk so he could that it was no longer recording. After placing the phone face down on the dining room table, Fowler returned to the couch across from Hawk.

"Thanks," Hawk said. "You sure are paranoid."

"And I have good reason to be," Fowler fired back. "I never revealed my identity to anyone, yet here you are sitting in my house. And quite frankly, it's a little intimidating."

"What do you think I came here to do, Mr. Fowler?"

"I don't know. Kill me? Anchor my body somewhere in the Potomac? Help me have an accidental drug overdose? I'm sure you have plenty of methods in your repertoire."

"First off, President Young has never asked me to do anything like that. I'm simply here to meet with you on his behalf and see if we can come to some sort of resolution."

"Any resolution that doesn't include the

American people learning the truth is a failed one."

"I understand your concern, but this situation is complicated."

"What's complicated about the truth? Daniels committed suicide. I saw it on the footage. Young can't get in trouble for this."

"You're a bright guy," Hawk said. "I think you can understand why now wouldn't be the best time to reveal the truth, even if it was something that the American people needed to know."

"This is *exactly* the time the American people need to know who President Young really is. They need to know the kind of man they're electing to the highest office in the land."

Hawk leaned forward. "Now, wait a minute. You said earlier that you weren't doing this for political reasons or that Young couldn't get in trouble for this. But what you just said sounds like your motivation is completely political. So, which is it?"

"Perhaps my motives are multi-pronged. I want people to know the truth, *and* I want voters to know who they're electing when it comes to Young."

"I'll be the first one to answer that for you— they'd be electing a damn fine man," Hawk said. "In fact, I don't know that there's a better man in Washington. But if you move forward with your threats to make this public before the election, before he's had a legitimate chance to address this issue in the totality that it deserves, you'll be ruining our country's chances at getting one of the best men who's ever darkened the doors at 1600 Pennsylvania Avenue."

Fowler sighed and shook his head. "I wish I could believe you."

"Your belief in what I'm saying is irrelevant when it comes to the truth."

"But that's all I want: the truth. And for some reason, neither you nor Vice Presi—President Young want to give it to me or the public. I happen to find that extremely disconcerting on so many levels."

Hawk sighed. "I'll tell you the truth about President Daniels. He was once a good man, but he became a victim of his own lust for power and control. At some point, he lost sight of who he was and why he wanted to serve this great country. As a result, he ventured down some ill-advised paths, made some bad decisions, and then made even worse decisions trying to atone for or cover up his previous bad decisions. When you combined each move that he made, it added up to a potentially disastrous result if someone didn't confront him and stop him. Yet he couldn't see that in the end and chose a coward's way out rather than face the consequences for his actions. And *that* is the truth."

Fowler cocked his head to one side. "Wait a

minute. You were there, weren't you, Max?"

Hawk furrowed his brow and stared at Fowler. "I was where?"

"You were there with Young and Daniels when he died. I knew you looked familiar. The glasses and fedora made it difficult, but I recognize you now."

"I'm afraid you're mistaken."

"No, I know I'm right. You were right there with him."

"I wasn't, but even if I was, it doesn't make any difference."

Fowler chuckled and shook his head. "Oh, no, I bet it makes a hell of a difference whether you were there or not. When this story comes out, those people who witnessed it but kept their mouths shut are all going to be crucified in the press—and rightfully so. You'll probably never work again in Washington, if you don't end up in prison somehow for helping perpetrate this lie."

"Never getting hired again in Washington wouldn't be the worst thing that could ever happen to me."

"I hope you didn't come by to quibble with me or convince me that keeping my mouth shut is for the good of the country because it won't work. I don't care why everything happened the way it did. I hate to keep beating this dead horse, but I just want the truth to come out."

"You don't care why everything happened the way that it did perhaps because you don't understand what I'm trying to tell you. Noah Young was the sole person who kept Conrad Daniels from turning the Oval Office into a throne room. If it wasn't for him—"

Fowler stood hastily. "I think it's *you* who doesn't understand. I've been more than patient with Vice Presi—President Young. Tell him if the truth surrounding President Daniels's death isn't revealed within the next forty-eight hours, the footage will go public. And I think we both know that damage control will be far more difficult then. Now, if you'll please show yourself out."

Hawk shook his head as he stood. "You're making a mistake, Mr. Fowler."

Fowler narrowed his eyes. "Is that a threat?"

"No, it's a fact. And I pray you come to your senses before it's too late. Quit being so unreasonable and accept the reality that sometimes the truth is complicated and messy."

"I don't care how messy or complicated it is," Fowler said. "The truth is important simply because it's the truth."

"Sometimes good men go astray, and exposing the depravity of their souls isn't always the best thing to do, even if it is the truth. Despite all his faults and flaws, President Daniels was still a person, a person who was loved and cared for by friends and family. Your quest to *expose* the truth about what happened surrounding Daniels's death will also require that the entire truth about his life be told as well. And I can assure you that such disclosure right now will *not* be good for the American people."

"And who made you the arbiter of what's best for America?"

Hawk strode toward the door before he stopped and turned to answer. "We live in a gray world, Mr. Fowler. When you realize that, you'll be much better off. The truth is still important, but it's not always a hill to die on."

Hawk touched the bill of his fedora and nodded at Fowler before exiting the house.

Fowler followed him outside but stopped at the doorstep. "Forty-eight hours, Mr. Summerton. Tell him he's got forty-eight hours."

CHAPTER 19

Andrews Air Force Base
Washington, D.C.

YOUSSEF NAWABI CRACKED his knuckles as he waited for the military police at the guard station to grant him access. He held up the security pass to Nawabi's face and compared the two. With an exasperated exhale, the guard trudged back to his post and picked up the phone.

Sweat beaded up on Nawabi's hands. As he eyed the guard's movement, Nawabi reached down next to his seat and grabbed his pistol. If he was going down without ever getting a shot off at President Young, Nawabi was going to take some people down with him.

After a few more tense seconds, the guard stepped out of his hut, raised the arm, and signaled for Nawabi to proceed. Nawabi slipped his hand off his gun and gripped the wheel. He eased forward, nodding politely to the guard who returned the gesture.

While Fazil had explained that great planning could always be spoiled by bad luck, he preached the importance of giving the mission the best chance at success. And advanced scouting was one of the pillars of Fazil's wisdom when it came to dealing a deathblow to the infidels. Nawabi took the instruction to heart, which was why he didn't question Brady Hawk's suggestion to visit the base ahead of time to get a better feel for it. However, Nawabi held everything else Hawk said suspect, including the suggestion to bring a weapon a day before and stash it somewhere.

Nawabi parked his car and got his weapons out of his truck, all disguised in boxes of office supplies. As he wheeled the dolly through the parking lot, he didn't notice any wary glances, which surprised him. He'd been told that everyone in America viewed anyone of apparent Middle Eastern descent as an enemy. While he hadn't experienced such blatantly rude acts in the general public, he certainly expected to garner them on a U.S. military base. Instead, he was met with friendly nods and waves from several people who passed him.

Focused on the mission, Nawabi didn't dwell on the friendly demeanor of the infidels. He had a job to do, not to mention the fact that someone who just flashed a welcoming smile also could've been the same person who authorized bombings over his homeland or even pulled the trigger on a jet.

They're all infidels, Youssef. They all deserve the same fate for the war they've started against Islam.

As he walked toward the last hangar, he kept his head down, denying even the slightest chance that he might be beguiled by the strangers' affable approach to him. Once he reached the hangar, he knocked on the door and prepared to give his speech as a deliveryman.

But no one answered. He waited for a couple minutes before picking the lock and entering the hangar.

The cavernous space inside was lit only by the sunlight eking through the opaque windows ringing the upper portion of the structure. A lone airplane occupied the hangar, though there was room for more if necessary. Nawabi ogled the technology surrounding the large tanker before snapping out of his trance.

Do your job, and do it well.

He hurried back to his stack of office supply boxes and maneuvered it toward a group of offices that rose three stories high. The top story appeared to have an access ladder emerge out of it, butting up against a hatch leading to the roof.

Removing the boxes from the dolly, Nawabi

opened each one carefully and reassembled his RPG along with the missile. He then picked the lock to the office on the ground floor and ascended to the third floor, where he used the ladder to navigate his way to the roof.

The sunlight momentarily blinded him as he climbed on top of the building. Hunched over to keep a low profile, Nawabi surveyed the area to find the optimum place to hide his weapon and take a shot. There were several ventilation fans located atop the structure that could serve both purposes. He eased his way over to the mechanism and hid his launcher. He proceeded to imagine what his activity leading up to the firing of his missile might look like.

As he closed his eyes, Nawabi saw Air Force One lurching skyward through the end of his sights on his RPG. He squeezed the trigger and watched as vicious flames engulfed the plane and sent it crashing to the earth.

Nawabi opened his eyes, satisfied with his accomplishment and looking for a quick way out if possible. There was little doubt that the base's military police would descend on the hangar, scouring it for any evidence.

The boxes!

Satisfied with his dry run, Nawabi scurried back down into the building and collected all the boxes before loading them onto the dolly. Once finished, he prepared to leave when he heard the clanging of keys just outside the door.

"Hey, Mitch," a man said. "Are you in there? I forgot my keys."

Nawabi didn't go anywhere. Instead, he crouched down low, waiting for the man to leave.

"Damn it, Mitch. This isn't funny. I know you're in there."

Nothing.

"Fine. I've got to get my keys. I grabbed the wrong set. I'll be right back. And your ass is mine for not opening the door for me."

Nawabi exhaled as he heard footsteps sound as if they were leaving the building. He gathered all evidence that he had even been there and crept toward the door. Opening it slowly, he stuck his head out to see if the coast was clear. Instead, he was startled by the appearance of a man right near the entrance.

"Gotcha!" the man yelled, his expression morphing from giddy excitement to disappointed bewilderment.

Nawabi jumped back, his eyes widening as he stared at the man.

"Oh, I'm sorry," the man said. "I thought Mitch was back from lunch, and I thought he was fooling around with me. I didn't mean to scare you."

Nawabi waved at the man dismissively. "It's no big deal. I'm fine."

"Hey, I don't think I know you," the man said. "Who are you again?"

"Just delivering some office supplies."

The man put his hands on his hips and cocked his head to one side. "Really? You were making a delivery? And who ordered these supplies?"

"I just dropped off some reams of paper like I was told."

The man eyed Nawabi carefully. "And who placed these orders?"

Nawabi shrugged. "I don't know, man. I just go where I'm told to go and drop off the supplies at the designated location. If you don't like it, you can take it up with my boss."

"I think I just might do that. Where's your card?"

"My card," Nawabi asked.

"You know, the one that tells me who you are and what you're doing here."

"Oh, my business card."

"You idiot. What kind of card did you think I was talking about?"

"Never mind," Nawabi said. "I must have left mine in the company van."

"In that case, I'm going to walk back with you to your van to make sure I get it so I can properly address this bizarre situation."

Nawabi took a deep breath. He had to do something differently now that this mystery man was demanding to speak with his supervisor.

"You know what?" Nawabi began. "I set my keys down inside when I was unloading the boxes. I need to get them before we head back over to the parking lot."

"I'm sticking with you, Mr.—"

"Reynolds," Nawabi said, offering his hand. "Arnold Reynolds."

"Mr. Reynolds, you better not be playing around with me because I don't appreciate this kind of activity in my hangar."

Nawabi waited until they had both reached the far corner of the building before he recoiled and delivered a brutal blow to the man. The man teetered back and forth until his eyes shut and he crumpled to the floor.

Snatching a nearby tarp, Nawabi placed the man on top of it. After securing the man's arms, legs, and mouth with duct tape, Nawabi rolled up the unsuspecting hangar supervisor. Nawabi worked quickly to cut out the bottoms of the boxes and use them to disguise the shrouded body on the dolly.

He wasted no time in exiting the hangar and headed straight back to his vehicle. He'd only walked about twenty meters away from the building when another man passed him before stopping and furrowing his brow.

"Did you see Dave in there?" the stranger asked.

Nawabi shrugged and kept moving forward. "I just made my delivery and left."

"That's strange."

Nawabi closed his eyes and said a little prayer that the man wouldn't become too curious.

Just go inside. I don't have room for two bodies in my trunk.

Nawabi didn't breathe until he was certain the man's footsteps were headed toward the hangar and not in pursuit.

Once Nawabi reached his car, he checked around to see if anyone was standing nearby. Satisfied the area was free from any prying eyes, he hustled to get the body into the trunk. Nawabi stored the dolly and headed for the exit.

The security guard gave a respectful nod to Nawabi as he drove past the guard gate and turned onto a surface street.

Though he had been caught up in the moment, Nawabi finally relaxed and remembered Fazil's sage advice about being prepared for anything. Nawabi had simply gone to get a feel for the place and make somewhat of a dry run. Instead, he had to knock a man out and sneak the body to his car. And later that night, Nawabi knew he'd have to kill a man, not the man he'd come to the U.S. to kill.

Nawabi thought it was a shame, too. As he reflected on every move he made while at the base, he remembered the man's face as one of the people who smiled and said hello.

Don't go soft, Youssef. He is an infidel.

Nawabi pulled out a picture of his dead brother and glanced at it for a second while stopped at a traffic light.

"Tomorrow, I will avenge your death, Abdul," Nawabi said. "I will kill the president—and then I will kill Brady Hawk."

CHAPTER 20

Zagros Mountains, Iraq

KARIF FAZIL RETURNED from Dubai, where he'd spent the day before getting all his financials in order since the latest influx of cash from Colton Industries, and slipped into his compound. Several leaders met him the minute he stepped inside and began briefing him on what had transpired during his time away. While Fazil told them all that he was eager to hear everything, he needed some time alone to gather his thoughts before everyone began downloading all their information to him.

"Will you people please just leave me alone for one second?" Fazil screamed in exasperation. "I need to think."

He slammed the door leading to his private office and collapsed into a chair. Setting up offshore accounts to manage all of Al Hasib's money stressed him out. If he had his druthers, he would have an accountant who could handle everything for him. But he didn't trust anyone. The last person he'd placed in charge of the cell's coffers bilked Al Hasib for two million dollars before temporarily vanishing to Mexico. Fazil took a special trip to Cabo to handle the thief. The news treated the accountant's beheading as another gruesome victim in the country's drug culture, claiming it was a skirmish between warring cartels. But those reports were falsified by Mexican law enforcement, likely because it was easier to handle the public relations nightmare of bickering drug families than it was to admit that terrorists were roaming free in their country. Making an example out of the accountant served a purpose for Fazil, yet it also meant more work. It had been two years since he'd handled the situation, and he still hadn't found the right person to take over the duties and doubted he ever would. The extra responsibility was starting to wear on him.

I only want to hear from Youssef.

"And you, too, Jafar," he said aloud. "Come over here."

The bird flitted across the room and landed on Fazil's desk. He grabbed a handful of crackers from the top left desk drawer and held them out for Jafar. The bird pecked Fazil's hand clean.

He looked at his phone, and there were no messages from his top missile launcher—and no reports of any terrorist arrest coming out of the U.S. The quieter, the better. If Youssef had been caught, Fazil knew it would be all over the news. President Young would use the report to show how he was making the country safe again, solidifying his position as the leading candidate when it came to stamping out terrorism. But there was no report, which meant everything had to be proceeding as scheduled. Nevertheless, Fazil still wanted to hear from Youssef.

After ten minutes, one of Fazil's lieutenants rapped on the door.

"I thought I said I needed some time alone to think," Fazil growled. "What part of that didn't you understand?"

"This is urgent, sir," the man said. "Extremely urgent."

"Come in," Fazil said, his tone betraying his mood.

The man entered the room and marched over to Fazil's desk, setting down a small black device. "I would not have bothered you with this unless it was absolutely necessary."

Fazil picked up the object and inspected it. "What is this?"

"We were hoping you could tell us," the man said. "One of the guards found this in a shoe from the cell floor where we're holding the two Americans."

Fazil opened his top drawer and removed a microscope. He studied the object for nearly half a minute before he set it back down and began to rummage through his desk again.

"What are you looking for, sir?" the man said. "Perhaps I could help."

"I am looking for a hammer," Fazil answered. "That is a homing beacon, and we need to smash it right now—and pray that the signal has not been activated."

"How can you tell if it's been activated?"

"You can't. The best thing for us to do is smash it and drop it in water."

Fazil continued to look for the hammer until he finally placed his hands on it.

"Time to take care of this," he said before smashing the black device to pieces. Fazil separated the pieces into several piles and kept them apart by throwing them into different garbage cans.

"I hope this thing hasn't given away our position," Fazil said. "Time will tell, but it doesn't look like it's been activated."

"In the meantime, is there something you want me to do to the prisoners as punishment?" the man asked.

Fazil flashed a mischievous grin. "Beef up security while I go handle the prisoners myself."

With a wave of his hand, he dismissed his lieutenant and dug into his desk drawer again. Fazil felt around until he put his hands on the bottle, his favorite Tennessee whiskey.

"If I'm going to beat some Americans, I should at least do it after drinking their whiskey, right Jafar?"

Fazil snatched a glass off his desk and threw back three straight shots before grabbing the whip from the back of his door and heading toward the holding cell. With Jafar perched on his shoulder, Fazil narrowed his eyes and refused to speak to anyone as he ambled toward his destination. One lieutenant tried to stop Fazil to ask a question, but he shoved the man against the wall and put a knife to his throat before releasing him.

"I am busy," Fazil roared as he continued on.

When he reached the prison cell, he jerked the door open and stumbled inside. He nearly slipped on the water that had pooled on the floor but regained his balance before tumbling.

Fazil approached Blunt first, placing the rope underneath his chin and forcing it upward.

"Are you comfortable in here?" Fazil asked.

Blunt remained silent.

"I know you are old, but your hearing is fine—that much I am sure of," Fazil said before giving a final shove to Blunt's face.

Fazil then stormed across the room to Alex. He stopped just short of her and eyed her closely.

"I hear you tried to bring contraband into the prison," Fazil said. "Gutsy move, but in the end it will only result in you getting punished far more severely."

Fazil stepped back and cracked his whip a couple times. He then called for the guard outside and asked him to release the prisoners from the bindings, first Alex then Blunt.

Fazil forced Alex to face the wall before raring back and snapping the rope at just the right point. The frayed ends of the rope grabbed her shirt and ripped it open. Two, three, four, five more cracks and Alex's back was bleeding, what was left of her blouse soaking up the blood. Once she was reattached to her chains, Fazil turned his attention to Blunt.

Fazil didn't hold back with Blunt, whipping him fifteen times. The last ten strikes managed to grab small chunks of his flesh. On the twelfth lick, Blunt collapsed to the floor, but Fazil demanded that he rise to or Alex would receive more lashes. Blunt stood and was promptly reattached to the chains for the remainder of his beating.

After Fazil was finished, he pulled out a flask and took several more swigs. He sauntered around the room and spoke in baby gibberish with Jafar until the Al Hasib leader decided to address his prisoners. "I wanted to share some wonderful news with you two tonight," he said. "Since you have been my hostages, you haven't received any news from the outside world and likely don't even know what day it is, so I thought I'd—"

"It's Friday," Alex blurted out.

"Someone thinks they know what day it is," Fazil said. "But congratulations, you're wrong. Two more licks."

Fazil didn't wait for her back to be turned. He simply recoiled and delivered three vicious shocks to Alex's legs. Her right pants leg was torn open, and blood spewed out.

"You are wrong," Fazil said, even though he knew she was right.

Psychological torture. This is the only way to do it.

"Now, as I was saying, I know you have not received any news from the outside world, so I thought I would deliver some to you directly. We could make this fun if I dressed as the singing telegram man, but I am not a pleasant person to listen to sing, and you have already had enough torture for today."

"The suspense is killing me," Alex said with a moan. "Out with it already."

"All systems are go for the destruction of your country tomorrow or, more specifically, for your president. Your loyal friend Brady Hawk has agreed to help me accomplish this plan. And fortunately for you, the little stunt you tried to pull with the homing beacon failed, so he will not be coming to rescue you. Instead, he will be helping one of my men shoot down Air Force One." He paused and sighed wistfully. "This is the moment we have all been waiting for, as we will strike back and get our revenge against the evil U.S. government."

"Ultimately, you'll find your revenge is completely unfulfilling," Alex said. "Once you get what you want, what will you do then? Make up more reasons and excuses to fight the Americans? Your battle will never end, and you know it. Not to mention that you haven't succeeded yet. I'd be careful about counting your chickens before they've hatched."

Fazil threw his head back and laughed. "*You* are trying to make me doubt myself and one of my best men? But like any attempts to prevent this from happening, you too have failed. The will of Allah will be done, and the leader of the infidels will be vanquished in a matter of hours."

Fazil tacked on a pair of lashes for both of his prisoners before exiting the cell and staggering down the hallway.

"You will wish you were never born by the time my men are finished with you."

* * *

BLUNT BLINKED TWICE and tried to clear the mixture of blood and sweat seeping into his eyes.

"Are you all right over there?" Blunt asked.

"Never better," Alex said.

"I know that's a lie."

"At this point, I don't really care. I'd almost rather him just end it."

Blunt struggled to take a deep breath. "Don't give up hope just yet. You never know what can happen."

"That's exactly why I want to give up hope, because what can happen is far worse than death. If Fazil lets his men do to me what they want, I promise you I will wish for a quick death. Just the thought—"

She quit midsentence, signaling to Blunt that she was losing hope.

"You've got to keep believing that we're going to get out of this, Alex. If you surrender any hope, Fazil has already won. Don't give him the satisfaction, no matter what happens."

"Weren't you the one who said you had given up and that you'd rather just die? You're confusing me."

"I thought about it some more. I just can't go out like this, not at the hands of this insane man. We've just got to stay alive and keep our wits about us. Do whatever it takes to keep breathing."

"That's easy for you to say. You're a man. They're not going to do to you what they're going to do to me."

"I wouldn't be so sure about that. But quite

frankly, it doesn't matter. I have faith that no matter what Fazil says, Hawk is going to somehow figure out a way to thwart the plans of Al Hasib."

"It certainly doesn't sound that way."

"Fazil is just playing mind games, Alex. I know this isn't the first time you've been held hostage, but it might be the first time you've been manipulated by a certifiable head case. He knows how to play the game, so you just need to learn how to play it along with him."

"What does that even mean?"

Blunt sighed. "Look, just don't give him the satisfaction of knowing that you've given up. Think of something—virtually anything—that could help you ignore all of Fazil's braggadocios claims. He's full of shit anyway. And I can't wait until his ace agent fails to do what Fazil is so certain will happen."

"In the end, it may not matter for us."

"Perhaps, but we can't let the picture that Fazil is trying to paint dictate our lives. If things go our way, we'll be out of here before you know it—and hopefully with designs on eliminating Karif Fazil and his terrorist organization for good."

"I'll try to stay positive, but I'm not making any promises."

"That's all I ask," Blunt said.

He winced from the pain, which still coursed throughout his entire body. He felt just like Alex felt,

but he wouldn't dare admit it, at least not to her. Someone needed to be strong. He figured it might as well
be him.

*Dear God, if you exist, please help Brady Hawk
tomorrow—and protect us.*

Blunt knew his prayer was self-serving, but he
didn't care. He knew they needed every bit of help
they could get.

CHAPTER 21

Washington, D.C.

THE EVENING BEFORE YOUNG'S FLIGHT to Texas, Hawk met with Young and his Secret Service detail to go over the specifics of the next afternoon's trip. While Hawk preferred another path, he didn't see one. If Young was going to survive, everything needed to go exactly as planned. Any variation would result in a tragic outcome, not only for Young and the aides surrounding him, but also for Alex and Blunt.

"If the Al Hasib agent doesn't get a shot off, two people are going to die for sure," Hawk said.

"And who's to say they're not going to die anyway?" one of the Secret Service agents asked. "This is all just a bunch of bullshit. We're all going to put our lives in harm's way so some old former senator on his last leg and some replaceable computer genius can survive—and even then, there are no guarantees. It's just ridiculous."

"They're my friends," Young snapped, "and there are no lengths we shouldn't go to in order to bring them back alive, even if the risk is high."

"These people are irrelevant," the agent snapped.

"These people have kept you safe in ways you can't even imagine," Young roared. "And we will do everything to ensure their safe return home, and that includes you."

The agent shrugged before slumping back into his chair.

"I hope no one else thinks they are a better tactical planner than the team of advisors here at the White House," Young said. "I've actually been out on the front lines, and I know the incredible value in having someone on your team who understands how to get things done. And while you may not see or hear about Alex and Senator Blunt in the news these days, I can promise you that they are the ones who are getting things done behind the scenes. Neither one of them cares about who gets the credit or the glory. They're all about making sure that this nation succeeds."

Young leaned back in his seat and took a deep breath before nodding at Hawk.

"Thank you, Mr. President," Hawk said. "We all appreciate your vote of confidence. And I understand why some of you might feel this is a dangerous game.

But this mission is more than just about rescuing two of our people—it's also about uncovering one of Al Hasib's hiding spots. If I can convince Karif Fazil that his agent was simply a bad shot, it extends our communication window with Fazil. And if we can find him, we can eliminate him once and for all. And as you all know, he's slippery."

"Except when he's walking free around the streets of New York," one of the Secret Service agents chided.

"He did have a nuclear bomb in his briefcase with a dead man's switch," Hawk fired back. "I wouldn't exactly call that *walking free around the streets of New York*."

"So, what's the plan?" another agent asked.

Hawk flipped over a large corkboard, revealing a detailed sketch of Andrews Air Force Base. He pushed a pin into the last hangar on the runway.

"The Al Hasib rocket man is going to be here," Hawk said, tapping the drawing for emphasis. "It's going to be a perfect spot to take a shot at Air Force One as it begins to climb, but it's a terrible location to shoot from if you want to disrupt anything else."

"Disrupt?" one of the agents said.

"Disrupt, kill, eliminate. I don't care what you call it, but that's what that Al Hasib agent is here to do. Their preference would be to kill Young—at least, that's their end goal. But I want to at least give off the illusion that I tried to help them."

"Fazil is no fool," Young said. "If his agent isn't successful, he's going to know you did something."

"Perhaps, but this should prolong the conversation with him. And if we're still talking, we can only hope that he still has the hostages alive and with him. Meanwhile, I'm still working on a way to find out the location of their camp."

"Back to the plan," one of the agents chimed in.

"I encouraged the Al Hasib agent to stash his weapon ahead of time," Hawk said. "And based off security logs I had pulled, he went there earlier today. I'm going to sabotage his missile launcher so that it will fire but miss badly. But we need to have a contingency plan in case things go awry and he decides to fire while the president and his aides are boarding Air Force One."

Hawk turned back to the sketch and inserted another pin.

"This is where the plane will be boarded. However, we're going to park a fuel tanker at an angle here so that the agent's view will be obstructed. Once everyone ascends the steps, they will proceed to the back of the plane and exit through the service entrance. From there, everyone will be loaded into a catering company truck, out of the agent's line of sight."

"Do the pilots know what they're in for on this flight?" an agent asked. "If this goes sideways, they're probably going to die."

"Air Force One can take off and land without anyone in the cockpit," Hawk continued. "It's one of the contingency plans in case something were to ever happen to both pilots. The plane can be flown remotely if necessary."

"Like a drone?"

"More or less," Hawk said.

"And how will you handle the Al Hasib agent?"

"I know his position. The moment he fires, I'm going to put a bullet in his head."

"How confident are you that this will work?" Young asked.

"If I thought that I was putting anyone in harm's way—real harm's way—I wouldn't do it. But I do think we'll be able to execute this plan and achieve all our objectives."

"You better be right," Young said. "My fate—and the fate of this republic—hangs in your ability to deliver."

"Don't worry, sir," Hawk said. "If I get a sense that something else is going wrong, we will abort everything. The cost of failure will be high, but I won't let it include your life or the lives of those around you."

"I find that somewhat reassuring," Young said. "I'm still a little uncomfortable with everything."

"That's how I feel every mission, sir. And things rarely go exactly as planned, but that's why we have contingencies."

Young dismissed the Secret Service agents but asked Hawk to stay behind. Once the last agent filed out of the room, Young sat in the chair directly across from Hawk.

"Are you really sure this is going to work?" Young asked again.

Hawk nodded confidently. "We're going to stop this agent and get Blunt and Alex back home."

"And Fazil?"

"I'm hoping I get a chance to take care of him. But if not now, soon. He's needed to be stopped for a long time. His threats are growing old and tiresome."

"I agree—I just hope that I can give you everything you need to be successful with Firestorm once I take over the office on a more permanent basis."

"I do, too, but there's still the issue of Jared Fowler's threat hanging over your head," Hawk said. "Have you given any thought to what you're going to do? The deadline is tomorrow evening."

Young stood and walked over to his desk. He grabbed a folder and handed it to Hawk before sitting back down.

"You know what's been bugging me about this whole ordeal?" Young asked.

"That some no-name guy who has no connections to Washington got his hands on that tape and seems to have no apparent agenda other than to throw the election into chaos?" Hawk said.

"Great minds think alike," Young said. "Those are almost my exact thoughts about Fowler. How did he come to get possession of this footage? And why demand that this be released right now? It's almost as if there has to be another explanation."

Hawk glanced down at the folder. "And I'm assuming that explanation is in here."

Young nodded. "The initial workup I had developed on Fowler was quick, a down and dirty look at the man. But I sent another agent back to do a more thorough job. I had plenty of unanswered questions, as did you. I needed to know who we were really dealing with and what was motivating him to do this *right now*."

"I'm assuming you uncovered something," Hawk said.

"Look for yourself," Young said.

Hawk gasped when he read the first line of the report. The name jumped off the page at him.

"I don't know if I even believe this," Hawk said. "His father is—

"Yes, believe it," Young said. "We now know the

missing link as it pertains to Fowler's motivation. The next question is what do we do with this information?"

Hawk smiled. "Leave it to me. I know exactly what needs to be done. I need to pay Fowler another visit."

CHAPTER 22

Washington, D.C.

YOUSSEF NAWABI SURVEYED the weapons cache sprawled across his hotel room desk. With his primary weapon already stowed on the base, he reviewed the rest with a careful eye. He wanted to make sure that when he fired a shot, it would stay true to the target. No jams. No excuses.

He cleaned all three guns four times and was about to move ahead with a fifth before he stopped. His mind was consumed with every motion he would take the next day. He visualized each step, each trigger pull. Escaping alive would be the real trick, though he didn't care if this was the end. He'd be with his brother Abdul in eternity. Advancing the cause of Al Hasib was an honorable final act, Nawabi concluded, and he would be rewarded accordingly.

Nawabi packed all his weapons and decided that

he needed to relax and enjoy himself on his last night on Earth. He took a shower and put on a pair of dress slacks and a button-down shirt before heading down the street in search of a nightclub.

The choices weren't plentiful, but he decided on a place named The Kabin Lounge. He eased inside and took a seat at the bar. After ordering a drink, he spun around in his chair to take in the club scene. Throngs of nubile women flooded the dance floor, pulsating in rhythm with the music. Guys jockeyed for position, snaking their way through the crowd in search of a willing partner. Nawabi treated the experience just like he would an assignment for Al Hasib—stake out the setting, make a choice that will give the best chance at success, and execute the mission.

While Nawabi pounded back several shots, he sought for the perfect target. He wanted to dance and let out some of his nervous angst. After several minutes—and two more drinks—he identified a woman of Middle Eastern descent. He wondered what she was doing here, especially without a head covering in public. But he decided to give her the benefit of the doubt before passing any judgment and chose to speak with her.

Nawabi wriggled and jostled his way through the dense pack of people attempting to dance. He had at least one drink spilled on the sleeve of his shirt, though he just dismissed the accident as a result of the packed confines. When another splash of alcohol collided with his chest, Nawabi grew mildly annoyed. However, he didn't go over the edge until the third incident, which had nothing to do with spilled drinks.

After a long journey, Nawabi connected with the woman he'd been eyeing for several minutes. She smiled coyly at him, more than accepting of his advances. She readily accepted his invitation to dance and began engaging with him as Zedd and Alessia Cara's "Stay" pumped over the sound system. Halfway through the song, however, another guy tapped Nawabi on the shoulder.

Nawabi ignored him. The second time the man tapped, Nawabi glanced over his shoulder.

"Can I help you?" Nawabi shouted.

"Yeah, you're dancing with my girl."

"What?" Nawabi said, arching his eyebrows and leaning closer as if he didn't hear.

"I said that you're dancing with my girl."

Nawabi turned back to look at the woman, who shrugged and winked at him. She then reached up and put her hands around Nawabi's neck.

"Are you sure?" Nawabi asked. "She's into me, not you."

"Listen, pal, you've got to the count of three to step away before I deck you right here and now."

Nawabi ignored the man, confident that he was bluffing. There was also the fact that the woman Nawabi had selected seemed fond of him. He tested his hunch by backing away from her, but she grabbed him tightly and pulled him toward her.

Nawabi didn't hear the first two counts, only the number three—a split second before a fist crashed into his face. Staggering backward, Nawabi tried to maintain his balance, but the combination of a surprise blow, alcoholic drinks, and flashing lights was too much to overcome. He crashed to the ground, toppling over a couple other dancers.

Before Nawabi could stand, a searing pain coursed through his midsection, compliments of the jealous man's right foot. Nawabi stumbled back down onto the floor and absorbed another blow followed by another.

Above him, the crowd roared. Everything was a blur to Nawabi, but he could hear some people pleading with the man to stop, while others egged him on and hoped for a fight. Nawabi noticed some of the dancers had pulled out their cell phones and were recording the encounter.

Deep breath, Youssef. It's not worth it.

Nawabi kept his head down and had decided to walk away—until the self-proclaimed boyfriend delivered a vicious hit to Nawabi's ribs. That was the act that changed his mind.

Staggering to his feet, Nawabi charged at the man and bowled him over. The crowd scattered as Nawabi refused to resist the rage that had welled within him.

All I wanted was a fun final night, but you had to ruin everything.

Nawabi pinned the man down by sitting on top of him before delivering upper cut after upper cut to his face.

The club security tore apart the man and Nawabi and forcefully led him to the alleyway exit. Nawabi grimaced in pain as he felt his ribs. He checked the corner of his mouth with his thumb, collecting a large spot of blood.

"Just settle down," one of the guards said. He turned to his companion. "Just go inside. I can handle this one."

Nawabi spit blood onto the pavement and muttered something in Arabic.

"What did you say to me?" the guard asked.

"I didn't say anything," Nawabi replied.

"Don't get smart with me. Were you praying to Allah or some stupid shit like that? Because it won't work. Allah isn't real."

Nawabi bent over, placing his hands on his knees while he tried to regain his level headedness.

"Where is the other guy?" Nawabi asked.

"Why? You were the one beating the shit out of him."

"He started it."

The guard shrugged. "Makes no difference to me. I just do what I'm told, and I was told to escort you out here until the police came."

Nawabi's eyes widened. "The police?"

"Yeah. Ever heard of them? They help maintain law and order in our country."

"I know about your police," Nawabi said. "I have watched videos where they shoot innocent people. No disrespect but I'm not going to wait around for them. I need to leave right now."

"Nobody is going to shoot you," the guard said. "But you better not run. They hate it when thugs run."

Nawabi spun on his heels and took two steps before he felt his shirt tugged into the opposite direction. He fought against the guard's grip but lost, tumbling to the ground. The guard put his knee into Nawabi's back and pressed down hard.

"What did I just tell you about running?" the guard said. "Did you take that as a personal challenge?"

With Nawabi's face pressed flat against the concrete, he tried to survey the situation. He had already observed the bouncer's beefy frame, comprised of bulky muscle. And if Nawabi had learned anything from his attempted break, he now knew that his captor was fleet-footed. Any designs Nawabi had on escaping would have to adapt to the situation. And the outlook seemed gloomy.

Nawabi tried to make small talk, which wasn't exactly easy with his face plastered against the ground.

"How often do you get to do this?" Nawabi asked.

"What? Toss drunk patrons out and hand them over to police? Almost every night."

"I am not drunk," Nawabi stated emphatically.

"Save it for the judge. Besides, I'm quite certain Mohammed would be disappointed in you right now."

Nawabi seethed and tried to ignore the comment, but he couldn't. "So you are an expert on Islam?"

"I know enough to know that you shouldn't be drinking," the guard said.

"Things aren't as black and white as your country would like for you to believe."

"My country? Hell, my country wants to open the floodgates and let everyone in. Half the people here would throw their arms around you people and try to hug you."

"*You people?* What does that mean?"

"Oh, come on. Don't tell me you're sensitive too. You know who I'm talking about—Muslims."

"And why do you think I'm Muslim?"

"It's not like you get to choose over there. It's either Muslim or they put a bullet in your head."

Nawabi craned his neck. "Is that what you think it's like in my part of the world?"

"Well, isn't it?"

Nawabi shook his head subtly and sighed. Before he could respond, sirens from a police car echoed in the alley, accompanied by flashing lights. The police car skidded to a stop a few feet away from Nawabi and the guard, both blinded by the headlights.

"Did someone call us?" asked an officer as he climbed out of the driver's side.

The guard jammed his knee more forcefully into Nawabi's back. "I've got a live one for you. Got quite a smart mouth on him, too."

The officer chuckled. "Well, we should be able to break him of that."

Before they could do anything else, the side door to the club flew open and a half dozen brawling patrons spilled out into the street. The men involved were swinging wildly, so much so that the guard stood, freeing Nawabi.

With the altercation demanding everyone's attention, Nawabi didn't waste any time making his getaway. He broke into a full sprint and darted down the alley. Checking back over his shoulder, he noticed one officer in pursuit. Nawabi ran a hundred meters before taking a sharp right and taking cover behind a dumpster.

The footfalls behind him grew louder as the trailing officer arrived in the area. He shined his flashlight toward the dumpster but concluded that the perp wasn't inside. Then he hesitated and went back to double check.

Nawabi's heart almost stopped as he watched the officer saunter in his direction. The guard picked up the lid and shined his light inside. He poked at the trash for a moment and then slammed the lid back down, apparently convinced that Nawabi wasn't inside.

The officer swept the area with his flashlight, but the beam never fell on Nawabi.

After a few long seconds, the officer meandered away.

Nawabi knew he had almost derailed his entire mission by being foolish. He hustled toward the street, appearing on the other side of the block from the Kabin Lounge. He hailed a cab and took the short ride home, if anything to avoid being seeing by the metro police.

He retreated to his room and closed the door, taking a deep breath. Fortunately, no irreparable damage had been done. But that didn't make Nawabi feel much better. He had tempted fate—and won.

Nawabi turned on the television, where the cable

news channel was covering the latest election story on the polls.

"Don't worry," Nawabi said aloud. "Everything will change tomorrow."

CHAPTER 23

Zagros Mountains, Iraq

KARIF FAZIL CHECKED THE TEXT message on his phone and smiled as he read it. Youssef Nawabi sent a note to let his boss know that everything was still ready to go the next day. In less than twenty-four hours, Nawabi would avenge his brother's death and fulfill his destiny by assassinating the President of the United States.

John Wilkes Booth will be forever trumped by Youssef Nawabi and Al Hasib.

The thought delighted Fazil, who grew more giddy as time passed. After years of trying to claim a victory on U.S. soil, Nawabi was going to deliver. Fazil clucked his tongue, summoning Jafar. The bird flitted over to his master and sat on his shoulder.

With a pair of hostages in his possession, Fazil's confidence in Hawk soared. The glorious moment that Fazil longed for was about to happen.

"Time to break out the good whiskey. What do you say, Jafar?"

Fazil poured himself a glass and danced around his office. He turned on his television and settled into his chair so he could laugh at the Americans.

One station led with the latest social media darling who was pregnant with her boyfriend of the month.

"These vapid people," Fazil said. "Someone must rescue them from this existence." He turned the channel.

The next station aired a story about a town torn apart by a racial epithet spray painted on the car of a high school teacher.

"They can't even get along with each other," Fazil said as he stroked Jafar. "How will they ever bond together to defeat their greatest enemy?"

Fazil threw his head back and laughed.

The next few channels weren't any better, depicting an athlete whining about how the league's owners were colluding to pay him less—*He makes twenty-five million dollars a year! What is his problem?*"—and a school teacher complaining about an administrator making too much.

It's all about the almighty American dollar. Tomorrow should wake them up a bit.

Bored of the subsequent shouting matches between new commentators, Fazil turned off his television, snatched his whiskey bottle from his desk, and staggered down the hall toward Alex and Blunt. Fazil wanted to gloat.

"I believe the two prisoners you inquired about are asleep," one of the guards said as he studied the security cameras.

"Good," Fazil roared. "All the more reason to wake them up."

Fazil trudged down the hallway leading to Alex and Blunt's cell. Fumbling for the right key, Fazil finally identified it and inserted it into the lock. The click granting him access echoed down the hallway.

As Fazil entered the room, he stomped in the puddle and announced his presence.

"It is time, my little infidels," Fazil began. "Time to watch your empire crumble. If only there was a television in here for you to see your president assassinated on national television, blown out of the sky. By the end of the day, the Air Force One explosion might surpass the space shuttle Challenger as the most infamous U.S. air tragedy. But unlike the NASA tragedy, I can promise you there will be people celebrating in the streets. A blow to the oppressive American regime will be dealt decisively."

Still facing the wall, Blunt grunted. "It's not going to happen."

"Excuse me," Fazil said as he strode over to Blunt. "What did you say?"

"It won't happen. Forget about it."

Fazil laughed. "Oh, but it will, old man. You see, your top agent is working hard to make sure that President Young and his plane goes up in a blaze of glory."

"I always believed you were an intelligent man, Mr. Fazil," Blunt began. "But now I know differently. You're arrogant and cocksure, but you aren't intelligent."

"*I'm* not intelligent?" Fazil asked as he placed his hand on his chest.

"Naïve or stupid," Blunt said. "You pick, mostly because nobody knows you better than you do. Now, which is it?"

Fazil balled his fist and recoiled before delivering a vicious body blow to Blunt. The old man coughed and struggled to get a deep breath.

"*That* is for being an antagonistic asshole," Fazil said. "Yes, I know enough of the English language to know what to call you."

"I've been called worse," Blunt said. "In fact, that doesn't even make my all-time top ten worst names I've been labeled by my enemies."

"If you're not careful, that will be the last name any of your enemies—or friends—calls you."

Blunt forced a laugh. "Look at you. Karif Fazil— a man born again and emboldened by coercing his foe to do his bidding, tasks you couldn't do yourself. Sounds like you have a promising future as long as Brady Hawk is working for you."

"That must sound familiar to you, too," Fazil said. "Without Hawk, you would have had nothing."

"If you think Brady Hawk is the only elite assassin available out there, you're sorely mistaken. There are others."

"But not that are Hawk's equal, are there?"

Blunt chuckled before responding. "Hawk might be the best, but there are others out there. Who knows? There might be one of those men sitting outside your cave here."

"If they are, they are sitting there with a bullet in their head. This place is one of the most secure locations in the world, with apologies to your NORAD base in Colorado, of course."

"I've been there—and this place doesn't begin to compare to NORAD."

"Perhaps not, but it definitely could be your grave."

Fazil turned toward Alex and meandered to her side of the room.

"I've never been to NORAD, but I know this place could use some chairs," she quipped.

"Ah, a woman with a sense of humor," Fazil said. "I like that in my women, among other things."

"Don't test me," she said. "I will break your neck, even as I'm shackled."

Fazil ran the back of his hand along the contours of Alex's body. "I'm sure you could."

"If it wouldn't get me killed and I had a way out, you'd already be dead."

With a wide grin on his face, Fazil nuzzled up next to Alex. "You sure are confident, especially for a woman."

In a lightning-fast move, Alex slid her left leg around Fazil's midsection and wrapped her right leg around him as well. As he struggled to escape her clutches, he slid down until his head rested between her calves. In another deft move, she squeezed around his neck until he passed out.

Fazil lay motionless on the ground for a half minute.

"Did you kill him?" Blunt asked, his face still turned toward the wall.

"I couldn't get enough torque to break his neck while dangling here like this," she said. "He's a big guy."

"Yeah and when he wakes up, he's going to be angry, big time."

"Do you think I care at this point?" Alex said. "Either Hawk rescues us or we die. It's really very simple."

"You never know, Alex. There could be another way."

"And what scenario would you dream up? A drone bomb killing everyone in this hideout except for us? One of Fazil's secret lovers sneaking in here and unlocking the door to help us escape? A giant meteor falling from the sky and killing everyone in this place except for us—oh, and this meteor has a pair of keys that help us unlock our chains?"

"Don't be so quick to shirk an idea you haven't thought of yet. *Something* could happen."

"And I could sprout wings, but that's not likely. We have to face the reality that we're probably going to die in here."

"Speak for yourself," Blunt said. "As much as I might have been ready to die after that last beating, I have a strong desire to live, if anything to make Fazil regret treating us the way he did."

"You're driven by revenge—so am I," Alex said. "But that doesn't change the fact that we have no foreseeable way out of here, nor do we have any allies within the ranks of Al Hasib."

"We might have one," Blunt said.

"One?"

"Never count Brady Hawk out."

Fazil moaned as he pushed himself up off the floor and staggered to his feet.

"You heard the man, didn't you?" Alex asked. "He's willing to betray his country to save us. I think we both know deep down that we're not going to make it, no matter what Hawk finally decides to do in the end. If he comes here, he'll be sealing his own fate."

"You think that, yet you've worked with Hawk on how many missions again?" Blunt asked.

Fazil squeezed his eyes shut and rubbed his temples before speaking. "Silence! We don't have time for this endless bickering. I will keep my word and not kill you or Hawk, though I'm not sure if I'll actually return you. If this works out the way I plan on it going, you might just survive. But until then—"

Fazil turned and drove his fist into Blunt's back. The old man wailed in pain.

"Tomorrow, it'll all be over with," Fazil said before marching across the room to Alex.

"Have a nice nap?" she asked.

Fazil grinned. "Oh, I have something very special planned for you after this whole thing is over. It involves about a dozen of my men. I think you may regret what you just did."

"Next time I will break your neck," she said.

Fazil stroked Alex's face. "See you soon, my dear."

He stomped in the puddle, splashing water on

both of them, before slamming the door shut. After locking the deadbolt, he sauntered down the hall and whistled Bruce Springsteen's *Born in the U.S.A.*

"Are you whistling what I think you're whistling?" the guard posted outside the holding area asked.

Fazil smiled. "It is. I must admit it is my guilty pleasure. The Boss is the best, even if he did come from the infidels homeland."

"But that song, it's so—"

"So American. It reminds me of why we're fighting them. They invade and attack for no reason. Tomorrow their entire nation will weep and mourn, paying a steep price for their intrusion into our world."

The guard flashed a wide grin at Fazil and gave a thumbs-up signal.

"The day we have been waiting for is almost here," Fazil said as he continued down the hall. "It is almost here."

Fazil fished his cell phone out of his pocket and responded with a text to Youssef Nawabi.

You will only get one shot tomorrow. Make it count.

CHAPTER 24

Washington, D.C.

THE DAWNING RED GLOW over the eastern sky-line chilled Hawk as he walked to his car. The west was still shrouded in darkness, still unstirred by morning's first light. The nip in the air forced Hawk to don his pair of gloves earlier than he'd anticipated, but he didn't mind. Keeping his fingerprints out of the FBI's database was always a preferred outcome.

Hawk climbed into his car and turned the ignition. The car purred as he pulled onto the street and headed toward Jared Fowler's office. Stroman and Associates had a better reputation in the city among real estate developers than most, but that wasn't saying much. The residents seemed torn between wanting more options inside the beltway and also wanting to keep the charm that made the capital what it was. Modernization was welcomed but only in moderation.

And over the years, developers earned a bad name for their overzealous building efforts.

From the revised workup Hawk received, Fowler was more or less a lackey at Stroman and Associates. Undoubtedly, his degree and collegial connections played a part in him landing an opportunity at one of the city's more successful firms. But there was another factor that Hawk couldn't discount, at least not after he learned the true identity of Jared Fowler.

Traffic ground to a halt, the result of a remodeling job on an apartment complex. One lane had been shut down, now occupied by long dumpsters collecting the archaic innards of a dilapidated building. With the sudden bottleneck, drivers honked and formed fists, shaking them at anyone affiliated with the project.

Typical Washington.

Ten minutes later, Hawk moved through the jam and continued on to Fowler's workplace. Fowler didn't appreciate the ambush at his home, so Hawk decided to approach the president's blackmailer in a more public setting. Hawk wasn't sure if this decision was the best, but he was pressed for time given that the afternoon required his full attention.

Hawk pulled into the parking garage and made his way to the lobby. A young, attractive woman greeted him with a smile from behind the welcome counter.

"May I help you?" she asked.

"I'm here to see Jared Fowler."

"Can I get your name?"

Hawk shook his head. "I'd rather not." He winked at her. "It's a surprise. We're old college buddies."

A wide grin spread across her face as she nodded knowingly. "Just give me a second."

Hawk leaned on the counter, listening in on the conversation. However, he watched carefully the button the woman pressed on her phone receiver. The name "Fowler" was accompanied by the number 314, telling Hawk what he really needed to know.

She hung up the phone and made a pouty face. "Mr. Fowler said he wasn't expecting anyone and he has some tight deadlines today. He wanted to know if there was anyone else you could speak with."

Hawk shook his head. "Now, I didn't go to college with anyone else but him, did I?"

She shrugged. "I suppose not. Maybe you can come back tomorrow?"

"Unfortunately, I'm leaving town tonight," he said. "I'm flying back to New York, and I don't really get here all that often. I'm sure he won't mind if I just pop in for a few minutes."

Hawk didn't wait for a response, following a man who was getting on the elevator a short way down the hall behind the receptionist.

"But, sir," she said. "I don't think that's a good idea. I—"

The doors slammed shut, effectively ending her protest. Hawk pushed the button for the third floor and nodded politely at the other passenger, who selected a higher floor.

When the door opened, Hawk exited confidently and began scanning the area for clues to where office number 314 was. Locating the group of offices in that section, he identified Fowler's and headed straight for it.

Fowler stared intently at spreadsheets stacked neatly on his desk before he stopped and looked up to see who was knocking on his open office door. His eyes narrowed when he noticed Hawk.

"What are you doing here?" Fowler asked. "Coming to my house was one thing, but now my workplace?"

Hawk stepped inside, closed the door behind him, and settled into the chair reserved for clients and guests alongside Fowler.

"I think you know what I'm doing here," Hawk said.

"I swear to God, I'll just release that footage right now. All it takes is one phone call."

"But then you wouldn't be a man of your word. Blackmailing the president is one thing, but then lying to him? I can't begin to—"

"I'm not blackmailing the president; I'm simply incentivizing him to tell the truth."

Hawk leaned back in his chair. "Whatever you need to tell yourself to live with yourself."

"I haven't asked for one red cent."

"You might want to look up the legal definition of blackmail because money doesn't have to be involved. Besides, we know that your self-proclaimed altruistic motives are bogus."

"Americans need to know the truth."

"I know, I know. I've heard your spiel, and it's tiring. And I've already explained to you why it would be detrimental to the public. You just need to let it go."

"My deadline still stands."

Hawk nodded subtly. "I figured as much, which is why I'm here to offer you a deal."

"A deal?"

"Yes, a deal. I know who you really are."

Fowler furrowed his brow. "Who I *really* am? What is that supposed to mean?"

"Don't play coy with me. You know what I'm talking about—I know who your father is."

"My father? You think that's going to persuade me to change my mind?"

Hawk leaned forward in his chair. "You know, I kept wondering what was your motivation for doing such a thing, much less how did you have the connections to get this footage. I know damn well you weren't there. But who has those kinds of ties and would be driven to compel the president to reveal the awful last minutes of Daniels's life? Why, none other than the son of Guy Hirschbeck."

Fowler glared at Hawk. "So you finally had a competent detective look into my past—congratulations. If you think you suddenly know me now because you know who my father is, you're sorely mistaken."

"Look, I get it. I believed I was the bastard son of a high-profile man at one time, too. I didn't want his last name either. But there was still a part of me who wanted to know more, certainly wanted to know more about his life and what made him tick. I always thought it would help me understand more about who I was."

"It didn't, did it?"

Hawk shook his head. "In the end, my case was different. He wasn't really my father, even though I believed him to be for years."

"Yet, here you are trying to act like we're the same, all for the purposes of what? So you can coerce me not to follow through with my promise?"

"Blackmail," Hawk corrected. "And, yes, I'm trying to make an appeal to you, though it's not what you think."

"Please do tell. This ought to be good."

"I know the truth about your father's death, about what really happened that night."

"Are you suggesting that it wasn't an accident? That maybe someone deliberately ran him off the road?"

"There's always more to the story. And I'll be more than willing to share it with you once you turn over that footage and drop your threats."

Fowler laughed. "You think I care enough about what that dirt bag of a man did to deserve an early exit from planet Earth? He'd already taken an early exit from my life—why would I even care?"

"Because you're human and you care about knowing the truth."

"I care about the truth being known regarding things that affect millions of people. My father? I couldn't care less."

"I find that hard to believe."

"Oh, do you? Well, Guy Hirschbeck was an absent father, a master manipulator, an oppressive authoritarian, and petty politician. Do I need to continue to demonstrate just how little I care about how he died or why? To be quite blunt, I'm glad he's gone. Whoever did this, did us a favor. My mother's never been happier. So, pardon me if I don't show the appropriate amount of interest in why my father is dead. I'm simply glad he is."

Hawk glanced down at Fowler's desk, desperately trying to steer the conversation in a way that could entice Fowler to surrender the footage. But Hawk drew a blank.

"Now, if you'll excuse me, I need to get back to work."

Hawk stood slowly. "For what it's worth, I know what it's like to be in your situation, growing up without a father and wondering if he ever thinks about you. It's not easy."

"You know what else isn't easy apparently? Telling the truth about why President Daniels died. And just like growing up without a father in your life, you still have to manage your situation, and not in a way that's always the most convenient for you. You do the best you can and let the chips fall where they may. President Young has less than twenty-four hours now to tell the truth and let the chips fall where they may with this election. Otherwise, his cover up is all anyone will be talking about for the days leading up to the election. And I can promise you that he's only going to lose votes."

"Thank you for your time," Hawk said. "I wish you'd reconsider. In the end, this is going to cost you dearly, including some prison time."

Fowler huffed a laugh through his nose. "You think anyone is gonna care about prosecuting me for exposing the truth about this? You're crazier than you look. Now, get out of my office before I have security come down here and throw your ass out."

Hawk turned toward the door and continued down the hallway, seething as he went. His trump card to get Fowler to give up the footage was summarily swept off the table and dismissed. Fowler didn't consider the offer, much less give it a second thought. The fact that he was Guy Hirschbeck's bastard son seemed more like a disgraceful detail in Fowler's past than a source of pride.

Hawk had misjudged Fowler's motives on every front. With time running out, Hawk needed a new approach—and he needed it quickly.

CHAPTER 25

AS HAWK PULLED OUT of the Stroman and Associates parking garage and back into Washington's deadlocked traffic, his phone rang. He glanced at the screen where the message of *unknown number* flashed at him. While his curiosity raged, Hawk hesitated before answering. If his past experience was any indication, the person on the other end of the line was someone he wished he'd never spoken to.

The phone vibrated and the screen blinked at him, both begging him to answer the call.

After a few more seconds, Hawk caved.

"Yeah," he said as he answered.

"Mr. Hawk? Is that you?" the man on the other end asked.

"Yes. Is this—"

"Kejal. Yes, it's me."

Hawk was taken aback by the revelation. Kejal's family harbored so much animosity toward Hawk, he couldn't believe they even mentioned that he'd called.

"Did your mother tell you I called?" Hawk asked.

"No one told me anything."

"Then how did you know to—"

"Your friends are in trouble," Kejal said, speaking rapidly. "Fazil is going to kill them no matter what happens."

"Whoa, whoa, whoa. Slow down, Kejal. Where are you?"

"I am in Iraq."

"Where exactly?"

"In the Zagros Mountains, northeast of Duhok near the Turkish border. I will text you the coordinates."

"And how are my friends being treated?"

"They are still alive. That is about the best I can say for them."

"Is Fazil the one torturing them?"

"Most likely, but I have not witnessed anything. Everything I have heard was second hand."

"And you're confident Fazil is going to kill them?"

"I heard from one of the guards that Fazil bragged that after the president is dead, the bodies of your friends will be dumped at your feet right before Fazil puts a bullet in your head."

"I will deal with this," Hawk said. "You stay safe

and avoid getting caught."

"Good luck, Mr. Hawk."

The line went dead. Seconds later, a text from Kejal popped up on Hawk's phone with the exact location of the hideout.

"The end is near, Karif Fazil," Hawk said aloud.

* * *

HAWK SPED TO ANDREWS AIR FORCE BASE, arriving just before 10:00 a.m. While Young's trip back to Texas had been scheduled weeks in advance, the activity level at the base seemed rather calm and usual, definitely not what Hawk expected to see so close to an Air Force One flight.

Hawk flashed his security badge to the guard and rolled through without a second glance. The lax security gave Hawk reason to be nervous, especially in the off chance that Fazil was using Hawk in more ways than one.

He parked and hustled toward the hangar that he'd suggested as the ideal location for taking a shot at the jet as it went airborne. When he arrived at the main entrance, the door was locked. Pressing his face against the window to see if anyone was inside, Hawk noticed all the lights were still out.

Hawk looked around for any other potential witnesses before jimmying open the lock and stealing inside. He scanned the area and tried to determine the best location for hiding a weapon the size of a missile launcher. Behind boxes on the ground floor wouldn't make sense as Youssef would have enough sense to know there might be base mechanics and supervisors inside who would make grabbing his weapon next to impossible.

To Hawk, there was only one place that made sense, the same place he would've hidden his weapon if this were his mission: the roof.

Hawk hustled up the ladder and broke through the hatch leading to the top of the hangar. Within a few minutes, Hawk noticed a large tarp bunched up and weighted down on the other side of the HVAC unit. He knelt next to it and uncovered the object.

Money!

Hawk held the weapon in his hands and peered through the scope. He turned on the tracking system and tinkered with the controls. Opening one of the screens, he recalibrated the missile-guided system software, rendering it virtually useless. To correct the problem, Youssef would either have to quickly recognize the error and know how to reprogram it or do a complete reinstall of the software. Based on what Hawk knew, he doubted Youssef possessed the technical skills necessary or that he would have the software and a way to re-upload it with him.

Hawk had just finished recalibrating the software and was about to stick the weapon back underneath the tarp when he heard creaking noise followed by a loud thud.

Youssef!

Hawk threw the tarp haphazardly over the missile launcher and scrambled on his knees toward the edge of the hangar. The HVAC unit provided Hawk a few seconds of cover, which is all he hoped he would need. If Youssef discovered Hawk on the roof, he knew it'd all be over.

Hawk slid over the edge, grabbing the ledge and hanging tight. Only Hawk's fingertips were visible, and he said a quick prayer underneath his breath that Youssef wouldn't notice.

After five minutes, Hawk's forearm muscles were burning so much that he briefly considered if he'd be able to escape without a broken leg if he dropped from such a height. He thought better of it and decided to persevere. But he couldn't simply hang forever.

Mustering all the strength he had left, Hawk pulled himself up so he was eye level with the hangar roof. He watched as Youssef recovered the missile launcher and stood. He glanced around for a second, which sent Hawk dropping down and out of sight. A few seconds later, a creak followed by a thud signaled that the coast was clear.

Hawk struggled to pull himself onto the roof and hoped Youssef wouldn't return, at least not for a while. Kicking at the tarp, Hawk felt to see if the weapon was still there—and it was.

Satisfied that all systems were still go, Hawk edged toward the hatch and crouched low. He peered over the edge and noticed Youssef toting a duffel bag and looking for a place in the area near the hangar to hide it.

"That bastard thinks he's going to be able to make a getaway today," Hawk muttered to himself as he shook his head. "He's got another thing coming."

CHAPTER 26

Andrews Air Force Base
Washington, D.C.

NOAH YOUNG FORCED a smile as he strode toward Air Force One. The small crowd of supporters wishing him farewell consisted of his support staff and several political allies. The rest of the people present were comprised of journalists assigned to capture Young's every move on the campaign trail. He took his time getting up the steps to board the jet, wondering if he should've put his life in Hawk's hands like he had.

The text message Young received earlier informed him that Jared Fowler still intended to proceed with the threat of releasing the footage. Young was disappointed but felt he must handle the situation in a different way, especially with the election so close. He'd placed a call to one of his confidantes and set a new plan into action.

However, Young found encouraging the news that Hawk had the coordinates for Karif Fazil's current hideout. That information prompted a short debate about whether or not they should proceed with the ruse of the flight and instead just send an elite black ops team in to rescue Blunt and Alex along with taking out Fazil. Hawk liked the idea but said they didn't have enough time to plan for a mission like that. He suggested they get some teams in place to capture Fazil in case he considered leaving.

When Young reached the top step, he turned around and waved. The entire scene felt staged, almost disingenuous. Of the people waving at him, all of them were paid to be there, in a manner of speaking. All campaign employees on the clock, engaged in their dutiful employment. He loathed such staged photo ops but accepted them as part of the political life. Spinning on his heels, Young headed inside the plane, striding toward the back.

A tanker was parked at an angle in front of the plane, obstructing the view of the terrorist, just enough that he wouldn't be able to see all the activity happening at the service entrance. The press couldn't see it either, which Young believed would be problematic once they witnessed a missile being fired at Air Force One. But Young's communication director prepared a memo that would be passed out almost immediately after the event. Young raised the issue with Hawk about the possibility of the Al Hasib agent shooting into the crowd when the plane was still on the ground, but Hawk assured Young that Al Hasib wanted every single camera available to capture their moment of glory.

Hidden from view, Young descended the steps at the service entrance and boarded a delivery truck, joining the rest of his team who had taken the same route. Once Young was inside, one of the base personnel secured the doors and then the truck drove off.

Young watched the rest of the scene from the safety of another hangar with an unobstructed view of the base airport. With a pair of dummy pilots occupying the cockpit, Air Force One rolled down the tarmac, getting in position to take off. Seconds later, the engines roared and the plane sped down the runway, prepared to lurch skyward.

This better work, Hawk.

Once Air Force One reached the optimum speed for takeoff, the nose of the jet turned upward as it lifted off the ground.

* * *

HAWK PEERED THROUGH his binoculars at Youssef Nawabi, who was using the HVAC unit on roof of the hangar as cover. But Hawk was lying prone on top of the base traffic control tower, high enough above the rest of the structures at the airfield that Nawabi couldn't actually hide. He was exposed, which was all that mattered.

"How are things looking up there, Hawk?" asked Will Baker, the Secret Service agent coordinating the day's security.

Hawk adjusted his earpiece. "I've got the target scoped in."

"And you're sure you've messed with the missile guidance system on the weapon enough that it'll totally miss?"

"Roger that. Our target couldn't hit the broadside of a barn from a hundred meters after I messed with the launcher's programming."

"Good because those planes aren't cheap. I'm sure the taxpayers will appreciate making sure that Air Force One doesn't get blown out of the sky, even if the president isn't on it."

"Just doing my part," Hawk said.

He watched as Air Force One commenced take-off procedure. The jet sped down the runway before it took flight. Though more than a quarter of a mile of runway before the plane reached the final hangar, it didn't take long to get there. Hawk watched as Nawabi steadied the weapon on his shoulder and took aim.

Trailed by a stream of smoke, a missile raced toward the plane before falling harmlessly to the ground. The fiery explosion caused a stir among the press corps capturing the event, a buzz so loud that Hawk could hear them from his position.

In the aftermath of the shot, Nawabi disappeared.

"Hawk, do you still have your shot?" Baker asked.

"I can't see him."

"What do you mean you can't see him?"

"I mean, he's gone."

"He couldn't just vanish."

"Well, I had him scoped in just before the shot. And once he fired, he slid back behind the HVAC for cover. I could see the upper half of his body before that. Now, I've got zip."

* * *

YOUSSEF NAWABI TOOK a deep breath as he watched Air Force One zoom in his direction. He steadied the missile launcher on his shoulder, checked all the settings, and stole a quick glance around. He didn't see anyone else nearby who could see him, but he didn't take any comfort in that. The moment he squeezed the trigger, he was likely dead. He wasn't sure he'd even live to see everything he'd worked for come to fruition. Another long exhale and he trained his weapon on the end of the runway.

This is for you, Abdul.

Air Force One's nose tilted skyward as it left the ground in a hurry. Nawabi took aim and squeezed the trigger, the jolt from the launcher sending him tumbling backward. The missile rushed toward the target.

Knocked on his butt, Nawabi sat and watched as his shot petered out and fell harmlessly onto the grassy area between the two landing strips.

What the—

Nawabi looked at his gun, studying all the controls. Everything appeared to be in order. There was no reason why he should've missed, not from this distance, not with a weapon that had a guidance system. But he had. It didn't take long for the fact to sink in that he had failed, sacrificing his entire life for nothing.

If I am going to die, I should at least take some infidels with me.

Nawabi picked up his missile launcher. Though he would have to shoot without a guidance system, he didn't think it would matter much since the last one offered him no assistance in nailing his target.

He turned toward the crowd of staffers and reporters still milling around near where President Young had boarded his jet. Nawabi was confident his training would help him connect.

One more shot, Abdul. And I promise to make this one count.

* * *

"WE'VE GOT A PROBLEM," Hawk said into his com unit. "I still don't see the shooter."

"Where else could he be than hiding up on the roof?"

"Earlier when I was sabotaging his weapon, I eased to the ledge and was holding on by my finger-tips. If he had a rope attached over there somewhere, he could've slinked away and repelled down."

"What's your gut say?"

Hawk sighed. "I think he's still there. He knew this was a suicide mission. And unless he got cold feet for some reason, I can't see him changing his mind."

"Let me see if I can get someone else to verify his location. We don't want this turning into a disaster."

Hawk peered through his scope, searching for any type of movement.

Then he saw something. It was just a flicker of light that came from an object the roof, but he understood that Nawabi was still on top of the hangar and active.

"I know he's still there," Hawk said. "Just saw movement."

"Should we send any men up?" Baker asked.

"Not yet," Hawk said. "I'd rather take care of this as discreetly as possible. I'm sure everyone on the ground is already freaking out about a missile missing Air Force One and exploding."

"A public execution of sorts might send a strong message," Baker said. "If you want to wait—"

"My friends' lives hang in the balance here," Hawk said with a growl. "I'm not interested in humiliating the enemy just yet. It'd result in the kind of retaliation that would mean two good people would lose their lives over this."

"They're probably going to lose their lives no matter what, if we're being honest about it."

"You could be right, but it's a foregone conclusion if we light this asshole up and every television crew in America films it and pumps it around the world. Let me handle this."

As Hawk finished talking, he watched Nawabi stand, armed with another missile launcher. Only this time, Nawabi was taking aim at the crowd, which was near the tanker still parked on the tarmac.

"Oh, shit!" Hawk said. "Have everyone clear the area. The shooter is going after the crowd."

Hawk zeroed in on Nawabi and squeezed the trigger.

When Hawk saw the stream of smoke trailing behind the missile, his heart sank. In the rush to get a shot off, he wasn't sure if he'd hit his target before Nawabi fired.

As Hawk watched through the scope, he confirmed a direct hit on Nawabi. A bullet tore through his head, and he collapsed almost immediately.

Hawk heard an explosion and glanced back toward the area where Nawabi had been aiming. Instead of seeing a roaring blaze of fire and a scene of death and mayhem, Hawk watched another missile burnout harmlessly on the grass, several hundred meters away from the plane.

Hawk sighed in relief, realizing that his bullet must've rocked Nawabi just as he was firing his weapon.

The press corps scattered for cover, and members of the Secret Service detail rushed in to secure the area. In a matter of minutes, the Secret Service confirmed to the press that the incident was that of a lone shooter and that he was confirmed dead.

But Hawk knew his biggest challenge remained ahead.

CHAPTER 27

NOAH YOUNG WATCHED THE SCENE unfold in horror. Despite knowing about the missile attack in advance, Young still felt a sense of shock when it happened. He also felt a sudden doubt that he should be pursuing the office of the president, which would guarantee more situations like this in the future. But the rogue missile fired at the crowd shook Young to his core.

After Baker briefed Young on what occurred just moments afterward, he dialed Hawk's number to get a less-filtered account.

"What the hell was going on out there?" Young asked once Hawk answered.

"Sir, I apologize for that scare," Hawk said. "Based on all my intel, I believed that we had every angle locked down. And of course, the one I didn't conceive of was the one that happened."

"How could you not conceive that he wouldn't

bring another weapon?"

"I considered that he might bring a long-range weapon, maybe even a semi-automatic gun to make a last stand. But another missile launcher?"

"How did you miss that?"

"I saw he had another bag, but I assumed it was his getaway bag."

Young clenched his fists as he spoke. "That was almost a costly assumption."

"I know, sir. Navigating these scenarios is always tricky."

"Well, I'm grateful nobody ended up dying, but it does mean I'm gonna have to answer plenty of questions that I'd rather ignore."

"I'm sure you can spin this thing in your favor, telling the American people that if the terrorists don't like you, then you must be the right man for the job."

Young forced a chuckle. "You've never been in politics, have you?"

"I ran for vice president of my class once in high school."

"Did you win?"

"Lost on account of the fact that I couldn't cut a ribbon that I used as a prop for in my tongue-in-cheek speech. I mentioned how I could fill in for the class president when he couldn't make ribbon-cutting ceremonies. I grabbed my scissors and after languishing for about fifteen seconds without being able to cut the ribbon I held up, I threw the scissors down on the table and walked off. I said something like, 'I guess I can't cut it.'"

"That explains a lot."

"If I'd used sharper scissors, I think I would've won."

"What was your campaign slogan?"

"'Vote Brady—the one who'll watch over you like a Hawk.'"

"That was bad, though not as bad as your screw-up today."

"I know it wasn't ideal, but at least we escaped without anyone even getting injured—well, other than the guy who deserved it."

"Where do you go from here? I'm assuming Blunt and Alex are still being held by Fazil."

"One of my contacts came through this morning. I'm heading over to Hyde Field once I debrief Baker. Thomas Colton has a jet gassed up and ready for me to go to Iraq to evac Blunt and Alex out of there."

"And you're confident you're going to succeed?"

"General Fortner is providing some support and has special ops in place."

"That isn't what I asked because I sure as hell don't want to have to explain another inexplicable event so close to the election."

Hawk was silent for a few seconds. "If I don't try, they're as good as dead. And I won't allow my team to die without fighting for them."

"You're a good man, Brady Hawk. Despite this situation nearly going fubar today, I have to say that I'm glad you're watching out not only over me but also the rest of this nation. Keep up the good work."

"Just doing my job, sir. And on that note, I need to get going."

Young took a deep breath. "Wait. Before you go, I have one more question for you. What about our other situation you were running interference for me on? Any development there? I really need some good news."

"I'm afraid I don't have any for you," Hawk said. "I made my appeal, even pitched him the possibility of learning the truth about his father's death. But he wouldn't bite and reminded me that the deadline was fast approaching later today."

"So, now what?"

"It looks like you're gonna have to do what you could've done in the first place, which is tell the truth to the American people. I know I'm not a political strategist, but I'm quite certain you'd rather be out in front of this story than trying to explain it after it already happened, especially so close to the election. It's all anyone would talk about all weekend long."

"I was afraid you were going to say that."

"He's got you over a barrel, sir. At this point, you've got to cut your losses and hope for the best. Besides, I think after today, you'll definitely gather a large portion of undecided voters who will grant you sympathy votes."

"I'll think about it."

"Don't mull it over too long because I think Fowler was serious. He's going to spill the beans if you don't."

"Good luck, Hawk. And thanks for everything."

"Roger that. It's been a pleasure to serve you, sir. Hopefully when we speak again, you'll have a more permanent title of president in front of your name."

Young hung up and exhaled slowly. He had dodged a pair of missiles, but a political bullet was headed straight for him—and the only thing he could do about it was to face it head on.

CHAPTER 28

HAWK SKIDDED TO A STOP near the hangar assigned to Colton Industries' jet and grabbed his gear out of the back. He hustled toward the plane, stopping for a brief conversation with Thomas Colton.

"I'm really sorry about all this mess," Colton said.

"Don't apologize to me," Hawk said. "This isn't your fault. Fazil is the one doing all this."

"I loaded you up with some of our best tech, stuff that hasn't even hit the market yet. I hope that helps."

"Between that and some special forces General Fortner has in place, that should be enough to get the job done."

Colton offered his hand, which Hawk gripped firmly and shook. "Good luck, son."

Hawk shot him a sideways glance but didn't say anything.

"Sorry, old habits are hard to break. For what it's

worth, I still think of you that way."

"Don't worry about it," Hawk muttered. "And I'll take all the luck I can get."

Hawk boarded the jet, and within a matter of minutes, they were airborne. During the flight, he reviewed all the tech gadgets Colton left. Some of the items seemed helpful—a laser cutter the size of a keychain that could rip through steel—and others not so much, like the wifi microphone pen that could capture conversations and beam them to an Internet server anywhere in the world. Hawk couldn't imagine a need for the latter on this mission, though he figured it might come in handy for a future operation.

The flight to Erbil took just over eleven hours, most of which Hawk slept. As the plane taxied, he checked his phone for messages, which included several from an unknown number and corresponded with several voice messages left by Fazil. All of them were angry and threatening.

Once Hawk deplaned, he grabbed the appropriate devices supplied by Colton and headed toward the parking lot, where Fortner had arranged one of his special forces agents to get Hawk into position.

"Major Aaron Matthews," said the man standing in front of a tan Humvee. "It's a pleasure to meet you."

Hawk nodded and shook Matthews's hand.

"Delta Force," Hawk said, his eyes widening as

he noticed Matthews's squadron patch. "And here I thought the general was just sending me some run of the mill Rangers."

Matthews chuckled. "I tried to convince General Fortner and my squadron commander to let us handle this mission without you, but they insisted there wasn't anyone more perfect for the job than you. You must be one hell of a soldier."

"I'm familiar with Fazil and his protocols, which I need to brief you on during our trip," Hawk said. "And speaking of which, we need to get moving."

During the trip, Hawk relayed everything he had learned about the Al Hasib hideout from Kejal, including the most viable exit points. If Hawk hoped to rescue Blunt and Alex from the prison, he would need help, the kind of help that could redirect him should the situation demand a new course of action. Hawk figured the more Matthews knew, the better.

About an hour out from the location, Hawk's phone rang again. The words unknown caller flashed on his screen. Hawk surmised that either Fazil or Young was on the other end.

"This is Hawk."

"It is past time you answered," Fazil said. "I have been trying to reach you."

"I hope you're not upset with me about your agent's failed attempt to shoot down Air Force One. I gave him everything he needed to be successful, but it's not my fault that you sent an incompetent operative. Though, I can't say that I'm sorry he missed."

"Don't worry, Mr. Hawk. *Upset* isn't the word I would use to describe my feelings right now. *Livid* and *outraged* are two far more appropriate words to describe my state of being at the moment."

"Then you remember that I had nothing to do with it and only did everything to help your agent succeed during the operation. I directed him to the prime location to take a shot. I supplied him with takeoff times and Young's entire schedule for the day. It was foolproof."

"Nothing is foolproof, especially when you prey upon a young operative like Youssef, may Allah give him comfort."

Hawk furrowed his brow. "You can spin this any way you wish, but deep down you know that he was incapable of finishing the job. Perhaps that was your plan all along—send a man you know will fail in order to coerce me to actually do what your men are incapable of doing."

"I hope you realize your attempts to persuade me that you had nothing to do with Youssef's misfire have failed," Fazil said with a growl.

"What more could I have done? Pulled the trigger for him?"

"President Young was not on the plane, making your argument moot. Even if Youssef blasted the jet as he was trained to do, all that effort would have been for nothing—and that is all because of you."

"You still would have had the best recruiting video footage in the history of terrorism," Hawk countered. "Air Force One disintegrating in the sky after one of your agents fired a missile at it in Washington, D.C.? The beheading of a thousand government officials from the United States wouldn't be able to surpass such a glorious image."

"But Youssef missed. So for the moment, I am left with footage of an incompetent fool who had an easy shot but missed. Who will see that and be compelled to join?"

"Maybe someone who can actually make that shot. Maybe someone who you won't have to spend hours training. As much as you like to think you're different than the American government, you're exactly the same. You'll spin the outcome in a way that benefits you and your bottom line. Don't kid yourself. I'm sure you've already dreamed up these scenarios."

"No matter what I have planned next, none of it will make up for the way you sabotaged my plans with my shooter. I hope you know there will be consequences."

"And there will be consequences for you, too. Do

I need to remind you that you're not running the show here? You're simply throwing rocks at a tank that's about to run you over."

"You talk tough, especially for a man who is at my mercy when it comes to the lives of his closest friends."

Hawk seethed. "The minute they die, you know you're dead. I will gut you myself."

Fazil laughed. "Just like you did all those other times before when you had the chance? I think you are fooling yourself, Mr. Hawk. But I am done talking about this. Get a plane gassed up and ready to go. I want you to be in the air in one hour, and I will give you further instructions once you're airborne."

"I'll be waiting for your call." Hawk hung up and growled. "I swear if I see that bastard, I may empty my entire clip into him."

"Karif Fazil?" Matthews asked, his eyebrows arching.

"The one and only."

"Taking care of him would certainly be a feather in our cap, not to mention President Young's."

"I don't care who gets the credit. I just want Fazil dead. That man is toying with us and will continue to torture us until he's dead and buried."

Matthews eased his foot onto the gas pedal as the Humvee purred. "Let's see what we can do about that."

CHAPTER 29

Zagros Mountains, Iraq

HAWK SCANNED THE AREA surrounding the Al Hasib hideout. The Great Zab River wound lazily around the bend, almost an afterthought amidst the scenic vistas created by the Zagros Mountains. The sun hadn't set, but it disappeared behind the peaks more than an hour earlier. To Hawk, the conditions were perfect for a strike, one he hoped Fazil would've never anticipated.

Just as Hawk began to go over the final plan with the Delta Force team members, his phone rang.

"Where am I going?" Hawk asked as he answered the phone.

"Istanbul," Fazil said. "I will email you the coordinates."

Hawk glanced at his phone as the text arrived almost simultaneously. The numbers looked familiar to him.

"The Chamber's old headquarters—interesting choice of venue," Hawk said. "I've been there before, you know."

"Where you have been is of no concern to me," Fazil said. "The only thing that matters is if you will show up. If you fail to do so, I will kill your friends. Do you understand?"

"I do. See you soon." Hawk hung up and stuffed his phone in his pocket.

He returned his attention to the Delta Force team.

"We don't have much time," he said. "If Fazil is the kind of man I think he is, he's going to try to threaten my friends in front of me. Let's make sure he never gets that chance."

Matthews selected Bobby Wright and Jackson Quinn to accompany Hawk on the rescue mission inside the hideout. If Kejal's intel was accurate, Hawk's newly assembled team would have to fight their way past three levels of guards before reaching the prison cells. To get out, Hawk and company would have to work quickly to escape without several more legions of guards rushing over to help. While Hawk pondered what the odds of successfully completing such a mission would be, he figured that it didn't matter. There was no way in hell he was going to let Fazil use Alex and Blunt as leverage any longer. Something had to give—and whatever it was, it was going to give within the next hour.

Hawk bowed his head and said a quick prayer.

"You religious or something?" Quinn asked.

Hawk shook his head. "Not particularly, but I'll take all the help I can get on this mission. If there is a God up there, I know he'd be rooting for us."

Hawk nodded at his two companions and started moving toward the entrance to the cave. They crouched low as they hustled across the craggy terrain. Hawk went first, followed by Wright then Quinn.

"Think these bastards know what's coming for them?" Wright asked.

"I hope not," Hawk said.

Once they reached the gate, Hawk invoked the protocol for gaining entry as Kejal described. Rapping on the gate three times, then twice, followed by three more times, Hawk hoped that he'd remembered correctly.

A few seconds later, the gate swung open. Quinn and Wright entered first, taking down the guard in a matter of seconds, breaking his neck with a quick turn and tossing his body outside.

Hawk pulled the door shut behind him and re-took the lead. They wound around the dimly lit corridor and went straight for another fifty meters before they encountered their next wave of Al Hasib guards.

This time there were only two, both put down by shots from the handguns fitted with silencers. Hawk and company stepped over the bodies and continued to move toward their destination.

After another hundred meters and a serious of turns, a quartet of guards stood positioned outside the inner sanctum of the Al Hasib hideout—at least, that's how Kejal described it. Being outnumbered presented a bigger challenge to Hawk's team, but they were up for it.

Hawk fired first, hitting the guard in the center of his chest. The two guards flanking him didn't have a chance to react before Wright and Quinn immobilized them with one shot, ensuring they'd never move again with another bullet each. That left one guard, who had reacted quickly enough and sprinted in the opposite direction.

"We've got a runner," Hawk said, racing after the man.

The last thing Hawk wanted was to incur the influx of more guards.

He chased after the man, who had cut down another corridor. Hawk followed as close as possible but gave up after the man vanished into a sea of hallways and doors.

"Let's go," Quinn said over the coms. "We don't have time to chase down anyone else. We've gotta get the assets and get out of here as quickly as possible."

"Roger that," Hawk said as he stopped and hurried back to his companions.

They followed Kejal's instructions and came to the last set of guards they were supposed to encounter before the prison. Two armed men stood outside the door, standing at attention.

"You guys take these two," Hawk whispered. "I'll get to work on the lock."

With silencers on the end of their handguns, the two Delta Force team members dropped the guards. Hawk rushed up to the lock and fished out the laser cutter Colton had left on the plane. In a matter of seconds, Hawk sliced through the thick deadbolt and pushed the door open.

Wright stood still at the doorway, gesturing for Hawk to enter. "After you."

The holding rooms were clustered along a long corridor that wasn't directly lit by anything. Each cell had a small light in the corner that was just bright enough that someone could likely make out the contents of his or her cell but little else. Water leaked from pipes up and down the hallway, resulting in puddles throughout.

Hawk trained his gun forward and moved cautiously down the hall. Kejal had warned about the inaccuracy of his timetable when it came to guard schedules and other variables, such as intermittent roaming security personnel. In essence, Kejal promised nothing other than to get Hawk in position to save Blunt and Alex.

As Hawk passed each cell, he glanced inside to find them almost all empty. He found one occupied with a man who wore a headband around his keffiyeh that contained Al Hasib in Arabic. He was huddled in the corner and scraping the floor with a pebble, either unconcerned or unaware of the presence of Hawk and his team.

Hawk slipped past four more empty cells before reaching one with a woman, who looked like she was fortunate to even be alive. Her cloak was bloodied and her face partially wrapped. Her eyes were visible, and the area surrounding them appeared puffy and swollen as if she had been beaten by someone.

Hawk swallowed hard and braced for what he might see when he found Blunt and Alex. He motioned for Wright and Quinn to continue moving. They snuck past three more empty cells before Hawk found his two Firestorm partners.

Alex had a bruise over her left eye along with a cut that had scabbed over. Other than a few nicks on her arms and face, she didn't look nearly as disheveled as the woman Hawk had just seen.

"Hawk, is that you?" Alex asked in a weakened whisper.

"It's me," he said, rushing over to her.

"Oh, thank God," she said. "I kept thinking they were going to kill us today."

Hawk glanced across the cell at Blunt, whose body dangled, his arms chained to the wall.

"You all right, boss?" Hawk asked.

Blunt grunted before answering. "These damn terrorists don't know a thing. I feel like I've been captured by the most incompetent people on the planet. They sure as hell don't know how to treat a prisoner. Hanging me up by my arms? I swear these punks deserve everything they have coming to them."

Hawk nodded at Wright and Quinn, who propped up the elder statesman. Slicing through the metal bindings, Hawk freed both Alex and Blunt.

"How did you find us?" Alex asked.

"I don't want to talk about it now because of prying ears, but let's just say I had some help. Now, I'd love to catch up, but I'm afraid we may not have much time. We need to move right now."

Hawk motioned for everyone to follow. Stopping at the gate to the cell, he glanced left and then right before re-entering the hallway. One by one, the rest of the crew filed out with Alex and Blunt sandwiched between Hawk and the Delta Force team members.

"Do you have a weapon for me?" Alex asked.

Hawk pulled a gun from his belt and handed the

weapon to Alex, never once taking his eyes off the path in front of him.

"Don't use it unless you absolutely have to," Hawk said. "I don't want you signaling the cavalry."

"Roger that," she said, grimacing as she moved forward in a crouching position.

They crept toward the door and into the main hallway, stepping over the bodies of the guards. After several turns, Hawk and his team were within a hundred meters of the doorway to the outside, Hawk heard the thunder of footsteps.

"They know we're here," Hawk said. "We gotta move out."

As Hawk led his team around the corner, they were met by a slew of guards. He held out his hand, preventing anyone from surging past. Bullets pelted the walls around them.

"Is there any other way out of here?" Wright asked.

"I'm sure there is, but I wouldn't know how to find it," Hawk said.

"So, you're saying our only option is to go through these guards?"

Hawk nodded. "I'm afraid so."

"Well, let's not waste any more time talking about it," Quinn said as he tossed a smoke bomb around the corner and waited a beat before sprinting to the other side of the hallway.

Wright followed Quinn and before the smoke started to clear, they started chipping away at the men standing in their path. Bodies started to drop in a hail of bullets.

Less than a minute later, the smoke cleared. Hawk peered around the corner to see only five guards remaining. From a sheer numbers perspective, Hawk and his team were still fighting the odds. Despite giving a weapon to Alex, Hawk was sure she wouldn't be able to withstand much. And Blunt could barely raise his arms, much less aim a gun at someone firing at him.

Across the way, Quinn nodded at Hawk before hitting the guards with tear gas. As the men started to wilt under the gas, Quinn and Wright picked them off until there was nothing left but dead bodies.

Wright looked at Hawk and flashed a faint smile. "Major, Delta Force will need immediate extraction in less than a minute. Stand by."

They hustled through the lingering tear gas, coughing as they avoided the guards sprawled out on the floor. Hawk ushered everyone in front of him, choosing to take up the flank in case Al Hasib sent reinforcements.

They took another turn toward the final hallway when Hawk stopped, confident that he heard approaching footsteps.

"More are coming," Hawk shouted.

Everyone quickened their pace as they walked toward the door. Hawk's head was on a swivel, his gun trained on the unoccupied space behind him.

When they reached the door, Wright tugged on the handle. The door didn't budge.

"What the hell," Wright said, yanking repeatedly. Still, it wouldn't move.

"Let me try," Quinn said, whose attempts also failed.

"Where is your laser cutter?" Wright asked Hawk, who was still waiting for the troops behind them to arrive.

He dug into his pocket and flipped it to Wright. "Make it quick. They're almost here."

Wright sliced through the dead bolt that was locked in place. But there was no key, only an access pad that served as a way of keeping people in as well as out.

"Hurry it up," Hawk said. "I can hear them."

The lock split, and Wright pulled the handle. Floodlights poured through the crack, the sound of Delta Force Humvees rumbling just a few meters away.

Quinn exited first, followed by Alex. Wright prepared to walk out with Blunt, but he hadn't moved.

"Come on, Senator," Wright said. "We need to go now."

Blunt hobbled toward the door but froze when the sound of footsteps echoed in the hallway.

A dozen guards rounded the corner and raised their weapons. Wright grabbed at Blunt's shirt but missed. Shuffling backward toward the exit, Hawk started firing his gun, dropping several of the guards in front. But the ones in the back returned fire.

"Noooo!" Blunt screamed as he lunged in front of Hawk.

A bullet ripped through Blunt's chest as the old man crumpled into Hawk's arms. Wright held the door open as far as he could, utilizing it as a shield. Hawk dragged Blunt's body behind the door as the guards continued to fire.

"Come on, buddy," Hawk said as he dragged Blunt across the rocky ground. "Stay with me."

Two Delta Force team members rushed over to help Hawk hoist Blunt into the back of one of the Humvees. Wright pulled the door shut behind him and scrambled for cover. Two of the vehicles with gun mounts waited for the door to spring open before spraying the guards and staving off any designs they had on a counterattack.

Alex and Hawk climbed into the Humvee with Blunt before the entourage of vehicles roared away from the Al Hasib hideout. Hawk felt Blunt's wrist for a pulse while one of the medics on the Delta Force team worked to halt the bleeding.

The wheels bounced along the bumpy road, jarring them each time. A missile exploded a few meters away, and Hawk felt the searing heat through the window. Another missile fell harmlessly behind them.

"I think we're out of their range," Wright said. "We should have a rather pleasant ride back to the airfield. Only fifteen more minutes before we reach our chopper."

Hawk had already disengaged with the mission details, content to let Delta Force handle the rest. All he cared about was Blunt, who had yet to open his eyes or squeeze Hawk's hand.

"Just give me a sign," Hawk said.

He glanced over at Alex. With all she'd been through, he thought she might be numb to the whole situation, but tears streamed down her cheeks as she grabbed Blunt's other hand.

"You can't die on us," she said. "Not like this. Not now."

Satisfied that the bleeding had stopped, the medic tried to stabilize Blunt after determining his vitals were in disarray.

Hawk pursed his lips and narrowed his eyes. "I'm not letting you go out like this, taking a bullet for me. What were you thinking?"

The next few minutes were a blur for Hawk. He

barely remembered any of the ride or how he even found his way to the waiting helicopter. He squeezed his eyes shut, trying to hold back the tears. But he couldn't any longer, the dam breaking as the chopper lifted off the ground. Through bleary vision, he watched as two Delta Force team members worked on Blunt.

Hawk threw his head back and said a prayer.

CHAPTER 30

Landstuhl, Germany

HAWK GRABBED ALEX'S HAND as they sat at Blunt's bedside, hoping that he would soon wake up. Forty-eight hours had passed since they escaped Al Hasib's hideout, but Blunt's status hadn't changed. He remained unconscious, stable yet in serious condition. U.S. Army doctors at Landstuhl Regional Medical Center had managed to remove the bullet, which just missed his heart and several major arteries. They didn't foresee any further complications but remained skeptical that Blunt had the physical stamina necessary to recover from such trauma.

"He's a battle axe," said Blunt's attending physician, Dr. Nelson, as he looked over Blunt's medical chart. "He's definitely not going down without a fight."

"What do you mean?" Hawk asked.

"A man his age shouldn't survive something like this, but he's not giving up."

"You don't know the senator," Alex said.

"Actually, I do," Dr. Nelson said. "We were friends another lifetime ago. I shouldn't make such bold predictions, but if anyone is going to survive what he just went through, it's J.D."

"But you're not changing your prognosis?" Hawk asked.

"There's nothing to change until he does. But we'll keep him here as long as we need to until he wakes up and can walk out of here."

Hawk chuckled. "You know those two things will happen simultaneously, right? The moment he wakes up, he's gonna want to walk right out the front door."

Dr. Nelson smiled and winked. "We'll make sure he only leaves here if he's fit. Don't you worry."

"You're the one who needs to be worried, making claims like that," Hawk said. "He's become even slier in his old age."

"Somehow, I'm not surprised," Dr. Nelson said before he exited the room.

Alex looked at Hawk. "What are we gonna do without him?"

"This isn't the first time we've been faced with this situation," Hawk said. "Only this time, I know Blunt isn't faking anything."

"Without Blunt, do we even have Firestorm? What's waiting for us back in Washington if he—"

"Don't say it," Hawk said. "It's not gonna happen."

"But—"

"No. Just don't, okay? We've seen him pull through worse before. He'll pull through this time, too."

"Even if he does, Blunt won't live forever. We need to think about what happens after he's gone."

"What's gonna happen is we will continue to fight against all the evil forces trying to ruin our freedom, no matter where they come from. They may be in the Middle East or they may be in Russia or China or North Korea. Wherever they're attacking us from, it doesn't matter because you and I will do what we can to stop them."

"But what about *us*? What's *our* future going to look like?"

Hawk sighed. "If you're imagining that we'd get married, buy a house with a white picket fence, and fill it full of children, I think you're going to be disappointed."

"That's not my dream—at least not all of it."

Hawk arched his eyebrows. "Then what is part of your dream?"

She let go of his hand and wrapped her arms around him. "The part where we get married."

Hawk exhaled. "Phew. I was hoping you weren't going to say the part about a house with a white picket fence. I think we would definitely need something more sturdy than that."

Alex laughed and kissed Hawk.

Hawk was about to say something when a coughing noise from Blunt's bed startled both of them. Hawk and Alex both turned around.

"Why don't you two get your own damn room," Blunt grumbled.

Hawk leapt to his feet and rushed into the hallway. "He's awake! He's awake!"

"Do you have to announce it like that to the whole world, Hawk? I swear, sometimes I don't know about you."

A wide grin spread across Hawk's face. He shook his head and looked down at Blunt.

"You lost some blood, but I think that's about all you lost—certainly not your sense of humor or your sarcasm," Hawk said.

Dr. Nelson breezed into the room and started checking Blunt's vitals.

"How in the hell am I still alive if this guy is my doc?" Blunt asked.

Dr. Nelson smiled and then turned toward Hawk. "I think he's going to be just fine."

CHAPTER 31

Washington, D.C.

THE NEXT DAY, Hawk and Alex returned to Washington, satisfied Blunt would make a full recovery. There weren't any pressing matters to attend to, but they both wanted to be back in time for the election. Their future plans hinged on the outcome. If Firestorm was to continue, it would require a champion in the White House, something James Peterson would never be.

Hawk eased onto his couch to watch the returns with Alex. The rote reports rolled in, news networks calling states mere seconds after the polls closed with less than one percent of the precincts reporting.

"How do they do that?" Hawk asked. "I don't understand. Are there time travelers who deliver these results?"

"Beats me," Alex said. "But they only seem to do

it on the states that are locks for one party or the other. It's comical, if you ask me. I mean, if you live in those states, why even bother voting?"

Hawk glared at her. "We might fight now."

"What did I say?"

"These are some of the things we're out there battling for and trying to protect. You've been with me all over the world. You ought to know that even the seemingly insignificant freedoms we have should never be taken for granted. It's amazing what we can do in this country."

She chuckled and shook her head. "Based on your reaction, you would've thought I just advocated for a communist takeover."

Hawk was about to say something smart when the news anchor on television said something that caught his ear.

This election appeared to be in the bag for President Young, but the dramatic revelation about the lie told regarding Conrad Daniels's death seemed to have shaken things up a bit, at least in the minds of some voters.

A news report aired, recapping Young's revelation at a rally in Texas just hours after Al Hasib attempted to shoot down Air Force One. Young spoke to a packed house at AT&T Stadium in Arlington, a sea of faces barely visible through all the shimmering American flags being waved.

Hawk watched in awe as Young explained how President Daniels committed suicide due to a mental illness. Young recounted how doctors and other administration officials tried to stop Daniels, but he managed to elude several Secret Service members and escape to a place at Camp David where he slit his wrist before anyone could stop him. Young confessed that he was right there by Daniels's side as he died and wished things were different, but explained that out of respect to Daniels's family, Young didn't want to cast a dark shadow over Daniels's presidency and give people reason to question every decision made. Young shared how White House doctors were preparing to remove Daniels from office at the time, but he acted impulsively—and fatally.

The reporter then showed how the polling tightened in the days leading up to the election, many voters expressing skepticism over Young's story and over why the strange timing of the announcement.

"Still think he's going to win?" Alex asked.

"Why don't we pop in a Bollywood movie and relax?" Hawk suggested.

"And forego watching one of our precious freedoms? Never," Alex said.

Hawk sighed. "I just don't know if I can take this. I seriously thought nothing would happen to Young after he explained what happened."

"He didn't exactly tell the truth."

Hawk nodded. "I know. It's amazing how close to the truth it is though, yet so far from it."

"That's the best way to lie, isn't it? Just take one detail and twist it. That's how you stay alive when you're being interrogated by terrorists."

"Is that how you stayed alive?" Hawk asked.

Alex looked down. "They weren't interrogating me for answers. I stayed alive a different way."

"And how'd you do that?"

"I thought about you—about us. And I wasn't ready to give up that dream yet."

Hawk cocked his head to one side. "Seriously?"

She nodded. "All I could think about was that you were going to come for us, even though I had no idea how once I dropped that homing beacon and Fazil went nuts."

Hawk stood up. "Come here. I want to show you something."

He led Alex up to the balcony of his apartment. A table for two was set and prepared, complete with a chilled bottle of wine.

Alex covered her mouth with her hands. "When did you do this?"

"When you were taking a nap this afternoon," he said. "I didn't have time to bake anything, so I got some food from the store. But I hope you like it just the same."

"I do. I love it," she said, her mouth still agape.

"There's something else I want to show you, too."

Hawk dropped to one knee and opened a jewelry box containing a diamond ring. "Alex Duncan, will you marry me?"

She started crying as she nodded emphatically. "Of course, I will," she said between sniffles.

"While you were gone, all I thought about was how you were doing," Hawk said. "I still had my duties here, but every other waking moment I spent wondering how you were and dreaming about getting my hands on Karif Fazil for what he did to you. I hope I never lose you like that again."

"That makes two of us."

Hawk stood, and she leaped into his arms.

* * *

AFTER DINNER, they cleaned up and returned to Hawk's apartment to watch the results roll in. Just after midnight, one of the anchors came on the screen, the bumper music comprised of strong drumbeats signifying breaking news.

Our political analysts have just called the state of Arizona for Noah Young, which gives him enough electoral votes to win the presidency.

Hawk pumped his fist subtly. "Finally, I can go to bed."

Alex eyed him closely. "That seems like a rather muted celebration for someone who's job depended on who won."

Hawk smiled. "It just means we've got more work to do."

He got up and strode toward the stairs leading to his room but stopped when his phone rang.

"Unknown caller," she said, picking up the phone and waving it at him. "Who do you think it is?"

"It better not be either of the people you're thinking of. One has a country to run for another four years and the other one wants me dead."

"Any other guesses?"

"Give me that," Hawk said, taking the phone from her. He pressed the button to answer. "This is Hawk."

"I wanted to thank you for everything," said President Young.

"Well, sir, this is an honor that you would call me so soon after the news outlets are projecting you won the election, but don't you have better things to do?"

"The better things I have to do are keeping Americans safe and their freedoms intact from any outside interference. And that starts with you."

"I do what I can, but you're going to need more than Firestorm to keep those evil agents at bay."

"Yes, but there's one man who needs to be eliminated before I'll be able to sleep."

"I'm sure he's more than angry after we stormed in and rescued Alex and Blunt. He's going to try to retaliate."

"That's why I won't rest until I know he's dead and buried six feet under ground."

Hawk took a deep breath. "Well, thank you for your call, Mr. President, but I really need to go."

"And where exactly are you going now?"

"Mr. President, I'm going hunting."

THE END

ACKNOWLEDGMENTS

I am grateful to so many people who have helped with the creation of this project and the entire Brady Hawk series.

Krystal Wade has been a fantastic help in handling the editing of this book, and Dwight Kuhlman has produced another great audio version for your listening pleasure.

I would also like to thank my advance reader team for all their input in improving this book along with all the other readers who have enthusiastically embraced the story of Brady Hawk. Stay tuned ... there's more Brady Hawk coming soon.

ABOUT THE AUTHOR

R.J. PATTERSON is an award-winning writer living in southeastern Idaho. He first began his illustrious writing career as a sports journalist, recording his exploits on the soccer fields in England as a young boy. Then when his father told him that people would pay him to watch sports if he would write about what he saw, he went all in. He landed his first writing job at age 15 as a sports writer for a daily newspaper in Orangeburg, S.C. He later attended earned a degree in newspaper journalism from the University of Georgia, where he took a job covering high school sports for the award-winning *Athens Banner-Herald* and *Daily News*.

He later became the sports editor of *The Valdosta Daily Times* before working in the magazine world as an editor and freelance journalist. He has won numerous writing awards, including a national award for his investigative reporting on a sordid tale surrounding an NCAA investigation over the University of Georgia football program.

R.J. enjoys the great outdoors of the Northwest while living there with his wife and four children. He still follows sports closely. He also loves connecting with readers and would love to hear from you. To stay updated about future projects, connect with him over Facebook or on the inter-webs at www.RJPbooks.com and sign up for his newsletter to get deals and updates.

Made in the USA
Columbia, SC
17 November 2023